"Please don't," she begged.

"Don't what?"

"I collect that you were going to say something commonsensical and tedious such as, you kissed me only because you were overwhelmed by my gift."

It had been precisely the excuse that Trent had been about to offer, but now he demanded, "What gave you that notion?"

"Well, what were you going to say?" she charged. Her voice was like a caress, Trent thought, and there was such a look in her eyes. Her lips had never seemed more inviting. "What?" she challenged softly.

Trent couldn't help himself. He leaned forward toward her just as she leaned toward him. As though they had a mind of their own, his arms reached out to gather her to him once again. . . .

FAIR FORTUNE

Rebecca Ward

FAWCETT CREST • NEW YORK

A Fawcett Crest Book
Published by Ballantine Books
Copyright © 1989 by Maureen Wartski

Library of Congress Catalog Card Number: 89-91900

ISBN 0-449-21837-6

Manufactured in the United States of America

First Edition: February 1990

Chapter One

𝒯he Honorable George Montesque's round and usually genial face wore an anxious pucker as he addressed the brass knocker on the vast wooden door of an apartment on London's fashionable Stratton Street.

"Trent in, Weldon?" he inquired of the sedate individual who answered the knock.

The manservant bowed. "Good morning, Mr. Montesque. Mr. Trenton is at the moment conferring with his solicitor in the study. If you will be so kind as to step inside and wait?"

"Suppose I must." Montesque divested himself of gloves, hat, and walking stick, then, settling his coat of buff superfine around his comfortable middle, strolled into the small front parlor.

It was a pleasant chamber, warmed by a blazing fire as well as the pale April sun. Montesque moved past a mahogany sideboard cluttered with bottles and tankards, a box of cigars, a blue ceramic tobacco jar, several pipes, invitations and advertisements to cockfights and sparring contests, a black lace garter, and a lady's fan, and made for a grouping of leather armchairs arranged around the hearth.

In one of these armchairs sat a fair-haired,

long-faced gentleman. He was dressed for riding in a gray coat, buckskin breeches, and top boots, but his eyes were half closed as though he might fall asleep at any moment.

"Morning, Monty," he murmured. "Early for you, I think? Dashed late when Trent and I left you at White's last night, and you said you were going on to Boodles'. I thought you'd still be in bed."

Montesque laughed somewhat uneasily. "Weldon didn't tell me you were here, Button. What are you doing at Trent's at ten in the morning? Ain't civilized, calling on one's friends at ten. Ought to wait till eleven at the least."

Mr. Jermyn Butterworth yawned and contrived to look even more languid. "I'm here to witness Trent's putting his new grays through their paces. They are dashed fine goers." Suddenly he fixed his pale gray eyes on his rotund companion and added somewhat sternly, "It's no use bamming me, Monty, I know why you're here. I mean to say, you were badly dipped last night, and now you've come to put the touch on Trent."

Montesque did not deny this. "Got to tell you, Button, there ain't such a thing as justice. Went to Boodles' after I left you two. No luck there, nor at Pickering Place, neither. Something in what they say about the wheel."

Button studied his manicured hands while asking, "What wheel?" Montesque cast himself into an armchair, stretched his short legs toward the fire, and stared moodily at his Hessians. "The thingummy that Fortune is supposed to be spinning around all the time," he replied. "One moment, you're up—next moment, you're down. Round and round you go."

"But that sounds dashed uncomfortable," Button protested. "I wouldn't care for it by half, Monty, going round and round like that. I mean to say, you'd be bound to get dizzy and fall off sometime, and then where would you be? In the basket, that's where."

"Quite so," Montesque agreed gloomily.

A brief silence descended on the front parlor during which time Weldon glided in with a decanter of sherry. "I say, Weldon," Montesque exclaimed, "how long has Trent been in there with the dashed lawyer?"

Weldon's cough was discreet. "It has been some time, sir, since Mr. Palchard arrived. There has been some discussion concerning the terms of the late Earl of Longmarsh's will."

"That would be Trent's great-uncle," Button informed the bewildered Montesque. "You didn't know that, perhaps? He never met Trent but the once, when he was a little perisher—Trent, I mean, not Longmarsh—and it just goes to show you, Monty. Longmarsh had any amount of heirs, but they all pegged out, one by one. So Trent's the new Earl of Longmarsh."

"How do you know that?" Montesque challenged, and his friend begged him not to be sheep-brained.

"If Trent isn't in for the title, why would a legal fellow come and see him?" Button demanded.

"Something in that," Montesque allowed.

They were helping themselves to the sherry when voices were suddenly raised in the study. The door banged open and a small, spare, elderly gentleman shot out. There were angry spots of color on his cheeks, and his eyeglasses were balanced crookedly on the high bridge of his nose.

"Mr. Trenton, I advise caution and restraint," he cried.

An incensed voice from the study told him just what he could do with caution and restraint. Montesque tutted. "Trent sounds hipped, don't he? Think he's been shooting the cat?"

As he spoke, Mr. Kenneth Trenton strode out of his study. Though he did not look drunk, he was definitely agitated. His tall, athletic frame, swathed in a purple brocade dressing gown, was held as tensely as a whiplash. His dark hair, usually elegantly arranged à la Titus, looked to be standing on end. His green eyes blazed like a mountain cat's.

"Oh, I say," Montesque breathed.

"Mr. Trenton, as your legal adviser, I insist that you compose yourself." The elderly gentleman settled his spectacles firmly on his nose and drew himself up to his full five foot three. "The terms of your great-uncle's will are explicit. There are no loopholes. There is no redress. You have the choice of submitting to the terms of the will or of not doing so."

"I know that, Palchard," Trent gritted. "You've told me."

"If I may advise you as I advised your father before you, nothing will be gained by railing against fate. Nothing, sir!" Mr. Palchard donned the hat Weldon had been holding, threw his greatcoat about his shoulders, and perambulated toward the door. "I bid you good day, Mr. Trenton."

"Peevish old fidget," Button observed.

Trent turned his head and saw his friends. "So it's you," he growled. "What're you here for, Monty? If you mean to ask me for money, it's no use. I don't have any."

"Hang it, Trent, you are too kind-hearted for your own good," Montesque said with some heat. "I'll wager you lent Handerby the blunt he needed to stay out of Queer Street, didn't you? Shouldn't be so liberal with your capital. Not the thing at all."

Trent flung himself into an armchair. "Weldon, I need something to drink. Something with teeth in it."

As the manservant departed, Montesque continued, "Anyway, what do you mean you're short of blunt? Thought you came into an earldom. Or was that a hum?"

Trent bared white teeth in a savage grin. "I inherited, all right."

"I told you so," Button said to Montesque. Then a look of dismay crossed his long face. "Wait a minute. All that blather about terms . . . Trent, you don't have to—to go and marry some frightful female before you succeed to the earldom?"

"Worse!"

"What could be worse?"

Trent covered his face with his hands.

Montesque looked pained. "Should speak clearly, dear old boy. Diction's the thing. Thought you said 'work.' "

Trent withdrew his hands and said clearly, "Palchard tells me that by the terms of Longmarsh's will, I shall be penniless unless I go to work."

5

Button choked on the sherry he was drinking. Montesque's round blue eyes seemed in danger of popping out of his head. He asked feebly, "What kind of work, Trent? Know you're bookish. Don't mean it as an insult, give you my word, only you did go up to Oxford for a year or two. Does your great-uncle want you to become a solicitor?"

Trent sprang to his feet and began to pace around the room so rapidly that his dressing gown flapped about his long, muscular legs.

"Longmarsh, blast his filthy old hide, said that before I could inherit any of his money that isn't entailed I'd have to earn it. It comes to ten thousand a year. Without it, there's no way that I can keep the estate going." He took another turn about the room and added bitterly, "The first thing I have to do is go and live at Longmarsh."

"You have to l-live away from London?" stammered Button.

"For twelve months. During that time I have to work on the estate. And 'because of my love and skill with horses,' I'm to start as a groom."

His friends stared at him in speechless horror. Montesque moaned, "The old fellow must have been touched in the upper works!"

Trent came to a stop in front of the hearth. He seized a poker and stabbed at a log as though it were his great-uncle. "Not he," he said bitterly. "It was Rousseau."

"Don't know the blighter," Montesque said promptly. "Button don't know him, either. Funny sort of name. Who the deuce is Ruesow?"

"A Frenchman," Trent said briefly.

"There you are, then, Trent. Old fellow must

have been as queer as Dick's hatband if he hung about with foreigners. Er, what did this Frenchy want with Longmarsh?"

"He wrote books. My great-uncle read them and got a bee in his bonnet that all men are equal. He believed in the noble savage. Mind you," Trent continued, "I'm feeling pretty savage myself. I came close to telling Palchard to tear up the filthy will."

Button, who had been speechless for some time, warned feebly, "Don't do anything you'll regret, Trent."

His friend turned burning green eyes on him. "By the terms of the will, I'd have to be at Longmarsh next week."

"Next week!" exclaimed Button. Quite forgetting his languor, he added, "But I thought you'd arranged to go to Epping for that shooting match. And, Trent, I've been meaning to talk to you about Downsom. I mean to say, the fellow has been insupportable since he bought his matched pair. He needs a setdown and you're the one to give it to him. I'd even go so far as to suggest that you should engage him in a driving contest. Your team will make his look like puffers!"

"Hang Downsom and hang Epping, too," Trent exploded. "Don't you realize that Miss Jerryham will be in London next week?"

He did not have to elaborate. Both Button and Montesque knew that Trent's courtship of Sir Bartholomew Jerryham's youngest daughter had been a difficult one, for Lavinia Jerryham was the acclaimed beauty of the past season. She had hair that had been compared to the purest gold, eyes of a celestial blue, a complexion so pale as

7

to put lilies in the shade, an exquisitely slender waist, and a fat fortune. Many were the eligibles who languished at her feet, and it was the talk of the ton that when she had refused the Duke of Comfrey, he had sworn to shoot, hang, and strangle himself.

It did not surprise anyone that young Mr. Trenton's suit should be scorned by Sir Bartholomew and Lady Jerryham. As the son of the late Honorable James Trenton, a Devonshire gentleman, he was well connected but without title, land, and fortune. An independence left to Trent by his late father allowed him a fair annual income, but it was hardly enough to cover the costs of Trent's London lodgings, a stable of fine animals to grace his curricle, and the cash needed to rescue his friends from their debts. Certainly, he had little to offer a diamond of the first water like Lavinia Jerryham.

Yet Trent was well thought of. Though certainly no fashionable tulip, his masterly way of tying a cravat had caused much envy among the blades of the ton, who also considered him a nonpareil and a dashed good friend in a pinch. His handsome figure with its six feet of lean, broad-shouldered good looks, romantically arranged dark hair, and flashing green eyes had caused many ladies' hearts—and the eyelashes of the most exquisite among the demimonde—to flutter. And it was whispered that the incomparable Lavinia had looked more favorably on Trent than her mama had liked.

"She loves me," Trent informed his friends. "Or if she doesn't love me now, she will in time. But, hang it, by the terms of this will, I *have* no time. Just when the Season's starting, I'd have to leave London. Longmarsh is a least eighty miles away. Father took me there once—and once was more than enough. Curst flat place, I can tell you."

He began to describe the estate. "Nothing's doing there. Absolutely nothing. Acres of sheep and farmland, a trout brook or two, a ramshackle village—that's the extent of it. My nearest neighbor is a Lady Vere, Palchard says. She's a widow in her fifties—some vague, provincial tabby, I imagine. Her property abuts part of Longmarsh's estate."

Button had been looking thoughtful. Now he said, "Never mind all of that. You have got to think positively, Trent. With Longmarsh's lands, the title, *and* that ten thousand a year, Miss Jerryham's bound to look on you favorably."

Trent's eyes flashed dangerously as he informed Mr. Butterworth that Miss Lavinia Jerryham did not have a mercenary bone in her body.

"Gammon," Button retorted. "She's got a mother, hasn't she? Mothers are always interested in money. I mean to say, Trent, that if you become rich and propertied, Lady Jerryham will eat out of your hand. But you've got to inherit that money first."

Trent groaned. "Curse it if you aren't right. Lady Jerryham's a fire-eater, and no mistake. For Lavinia's sake then. But to be a dashed *groom!*" he added furiously. "I'll be expected to muck out the stables."

Montesque shuddered convulsively. "Horrible,

dear old boy. Beg you won't mention it. Hope you don't run into anybody we know."

"Hardly likely, is it? Besides, that miserable will forbids me to 'divulge my true identity' unless there's a dire emergency. As if I'd want anyone to know! I suppose," Trent concluded mournfully, "I should be thankful that nobody will realize who I am except the land steward, Howard Block."

Weldon appeared at that moment. He held a silver tray on which stood a crystal goblet. Trent grabbed it, swallowed, and made a face. "Lord, that's awful. What is it?"

"Lemonade, sir."

"Lemonade! Of all the cabbage-brained— I asked for something strong, didn't I?"

Weldon met his master's glare impassively. "It is unlikely that you will be served brandy or sherry at Longmarsh, sir. And the domestic help is never permitted to imbibe spirits while on duty. One must begin somewhere, sir, if I might make so bold."

Trent looked stricken. Montesque went up to him and put a pudgy arm around his friend's broad shoulders.

"It's the damned wheel, Trent." He sighed. "No help for it, dear old boy. Wheel goes round and round, and right now you're at the bottom of its swing. Mark my words, it's your turn to be in the basket."

Chapter Two

Young Peter Link, underfootman in the employ of Charlotte Choate, Lady Vere, held open the side door to Vere Hall and gave his deepest bow. This was odd in view of the fact that the young woman walking briskly along the ground-floor anteroom was obviously not one of the privileged ten thousand.

Though she moved with a grace that a queen might admire, her neat gray dress of unadorned muslin was not in its first youth and her bonnet was frankly ugly. Nor was the face framed by that dispirited bonnet one of matchless beauty. Though the young lady's large hazel eyes were uncommonly handsome and expressive, her nose was too pert to be modish, her hair an unstylish red-gold color, and the generous curve of her mouth did not even remotely resemble a cupid's bow. Even so, her smile made young Link feel as if the sun had suddenly burst through the clouds.

"I'm so grateful it has decided not to rain," she was saying.

Link glanced swiftly about. Seeing that the butler, Reddington, was nowhere is sight, he warned, "Well, Miss Margaret, you'd best be careful. It might still rain an' all. April weather's that changeable."

Margaret Hannay stepped through the door and tilted her face toward the gray sky. "But I can see the sun behind the clouds." She smiled again and added, "Thank you, Link, and good night."

The underfootman bowed once more and watched her walk down the stairs with her customary brisk step. It was as if Miss Margaret couldn't wait to leave Vere Hall, and no wonder. The poor young lady had been penned indoors all day with the mistress, who was as mean a squeeze-crab as ever lived. Run here, go there, take it back, I don't want it—*that* was my lady's style. And she treated her paid young companion like a slave.

This fact had drawn battle lines belowstairs. Reddington, the butler who had tyrannized Vere domestics for thirty years, was swift to follow his mistress's lead, and Lady Vere's Tyburn-faced dresser, Palley, did what she could to make Miss Margaret's life even more miserable. The other servants ranged themselves squarely on the young lady's side and admired the fact that no matter how badly Lady Vere abused her, she never lost her smile.

Margaret was smiling now—with anticipation. "Tea," she told herself hungrily, "with thick toast and a good cose with Mama. And I shan't have to see Lady Vere for fourteen more hours. What could be better?"

Humming to herself, she passed her employer's topiary garden and followed the path toward the bridge that spanned a trout stream. Beyond the bridge was a thicket of beech and alder trees that marked the end of Lady Vere's property and the beginning of the broad acreage that belonged to the Earl of Longmarsh.

"Bloody hell!"

The furious male voice exploded out of no-where and stopped Margaret dead in her tracks. She looked quickly about her but saw nothing.

"Oh, damn and confound this filthy thing to perdition," the voice roared. "I won't go on with it. Hell and the devil, I'm done!"

A wooden pole came hurtling out of the trees. It was followed immediately by the business end of a pitchfork. Next, a tall, broad-shouldered man erupted into view.

Quivering with indignation from the top of his dark head to the heels of his boots, the tall man aimed a kick at the pitchfork. He missed and nearly fell flat on his face. He looked so comical trying to regain his balance that Margaret, who had been about to take to her heels, laughed in-stead.

He turned and saw her. There was a dangerous glint in the green eyes that met hers, and she saw his fine mouth tighten. A braver heart than Margaret's might have quailed, except that the flushed and wrathful face now underwent a transformation. Anger drained away and was re-placed by embarrassment.

"Ah," he stammered. "Good—good afternoon, ma'am."

Margaret kept a wary eye on him as she re-turned the greeting. He continued to look flus-tered for a moment, then suddenly tipped back his head and laughed. He had a nice laugh, Margaret thought, deep and full.

"A proper fool I've made of myself," he exclaimed ruefully. "I don't wonder that you think I'm a bedlamite. I apologize for my language."

"It was colorful," she allowed.

He glared at the pitchfork on the ground. "I had provocation. I've broken this wretched thing again. It's the third pitchfork I've ruined this week."

Margaret was frankly puzzled. The man looked to be twenty-five or thereabouts, and he held his lean, well-muscled body with the powerful grace of a sportsman. His speech and manner proclaimed him to be a gentleman, but his scuffed, muddy boots and rough clothing were more fit for a laborer. And they appeared to have been made for a much smaller man.

He seemed to sense her confusion and a flush stained his sun-darkened cheeks. "Allow me to introduce myself, ma'am. I'm the new groom at Longmarsh."

Groom?

"Ken Trent, ma'am, at your service." He held himself ramrod straight as if he were facing a firing squad and bit off each word as if he personally hated it. Margaret gave herself a hard, mental shake. *Stop staring, widgeon!*

As though such meetings were commonplace, she said, "I am glad to make your acquaintance, Mr. Trent. I'm Margaret Hannay, companion to Lady Vere."

"Miss Hannay, your very obedient."

The words were spoken automatically as though he'd used them every day of his life, and the bow he gave her was most accomplished. Looking questioningly into his eyes, Margaret saw something there that reminded her of how she felt when she faced Lady Vere each morning.

Birds of a feather, she thought ruefully. Of course, he was a gentleman down on his luck. But why should such a person work as a groom, of all things? Surely there were more suitable occupations.

She tried to think of something to say. "Did you really break three pitchforks this week?" she managed.

He nodded. "Jennings—the head groom at Longmarsh—will have his revenge. He'll keep me mucking out the stables so that I can't tend to Beau as I should. Beau," he explained, "is a chestnut gelding. He used to be one of the old earl's favorite horses, and no wonder. He's Welsh bred—a real goer."

"What is the matter with him?"

"That da—that confounded fool, Jennings, *would* try to ride him. Beau threw him, and serve him right, except that in the process the horse grazed his foreleg. It's showing red."

She frowned, concerned. "You are fomenting it?"

What do you take me for? his green eyes accused. "Naturally. But we are out of spermaceti ointment," he added, wrathfully, "and Jennings as good as told me to mind my own business when I brought it to his attention."

Margaret was shocked. "But that is infamous! No groom worth his salt would allow—but, I collect, Mr. Jennings is *not* worth his salt." She thought for a moment, then added firmly, "It's obvious that you must be let free to attend Beau."

She stepped off the path and bent to examine the broken pitchfork. "You used string, that's why it would not hold. You need a leather thong. If you had one, I could show you how to mend it."

He looked nonplussed, so she explained, "I grew up in the country, in Shropshire. When I was a child, I thought the stable was the most fascinating place that ever was and even Mama's scolds couldn't keep me from helping our old groom, Russkin."

Trent digested this in astonished silence. He could not picture any of the ladies of his acquaintance recognizing a pitchfork, let alone knowing how to mend one.

"Russkin's philosophy was 'Do or do without.' It's helped me through more than one hard spot, I can tell you."

Trent reasoned that Longmarsh was in the country and that Miss Margaret Hannay was, after all, a lady's companion. He supposed that such young women needed to know all manner of things.

"Very sensible," he said heartily. "Look, Miss Hannay, if I nip back to the stable and get a thong from the stable, could you . . . ? I realize it'd be imposing on your kindness, but I'm up the River Tick. I'll be back in no time, if you'd wait."

But she was shaking her head. "Why make an unnecessary trip? I collect that the late earl's stable is a stone's throw from here. I'll walk over there with you, Mr. Trent."

His green eyes glowed with enthusiasm. "Famous! You're too kind, Miss Hannay." Then he paused and added frankly, "But my name's simply Trent, not 'Mr.' anything. At least, not—"

He broke off, but Margaret mentally supplied the rest of the sentence. *At least, not here.* "Well," she said, " 'Miss Hannay' will not do, either. I answer to Margaret."

She held out her hand as she spoke, and he took it. Expecting him to shake it, she was surprised when he bent over it. The powerful grace of the gesture, the practiced touch of cool, firm lips on her skin, suggested that Ken Trent had much practice in charming the ladies.

"This way, Miss Hannay," he said, offering her his arm. "You're right about the old—about the late earl's stables being nearby. Have you been with Lady Vere long?"

"Six months."

She had not sighed—Trent was sure of that—but there was a sigh in her words all the same. He looked down questioningly into the heart-shaped face, half hidden by the hideous bonnet, and gazed into brilliant hazel eyes.

Trent blinked. Until now he'd thought of Margaret Hannay as a pleasant but commonplace young woman. Now he saw that he'd been wrong. Even apart from her bright hair and a complexion that glowed with exercise, her eyes were extraordinary. Brimming with humor and character, they gave her face a quality that was too vivid to be fobbed off as mere beauty.

And she was gently born or he was no judge of anything. What on earth was she doing working as a paid companion—and in this uncivilized place?

He probed. "I don't know much about Lady

Vere, but what I've heard the servants say of her isn't complimentary." Completely forgetting his own status, he added loftily, "You know how *servants* talk. They say Lady Vere is a regular fire-eater."

Instead of reacting to this, Margaret exclaimed, "I see the stable now! It really is lovely."

"What, the stable?"

She smiled at his bewildered tone. "I mean all of Longmarsh. I think it is quite the handsomest estate I've seen."

Trent did not share her enthusiasm. In the ten days he'd languished in exile, it had done little else but rain, and he considered Longmarsh the most dreary, flat, and godforsaken place he'd ever had the misfortune to see. He had asked himself, a thousand times over, whether it was worth it to continue his unholy charade.

Always, one answer had come back. Lavinia Jerryham was worth any sacrifice.

"You *like* Longmarsh?" he inquired.

"My father used to talk about the kind of home we would have one day." A dreamy note had crept into Margaret's voice. "It was as if he were describing Longmarsh. Those sheep grazing in those hills and the trout brooks winding through the meadows like ribbons, and then the village, which is so peaceful, so *right*. I would have liked to live at Longmarsh-on-Hill, but Lady Vere said that Mama and I should take up residence in her cottage on the other side of these woods."

The late earl had owned several cottages that housed his favored retainers. They were sturdy, comfortable residences. Lady Vere's cottage, however, was a horse of a different color. Trent recalled passing it on his way to Longmarsh ten days ago, and a more dismal edifice he had seldom seen. It had looked ready to tumble down at the slightest provocation.

"Ah," he said lamely. "I see."

They walked in silence until they reached the stable. It was an imposing structure with a high ceiling. Behind it was a paddock for the earl's horses and separate quarters for the chief groom and his assistant.

The horses in their stalls had already been groomed and fed, but the stable badly needed mucking out. As Margaret looked about her, a tall, spirited bay gelding whickered reproachfully from one of the stalls.

Trent went to him at once. "There, Beau, old fellow, I'm back. You see," he went on, "what I mean about the foreleg. I've been so busy with it that I neglected my, ah, other duties."

"Where is Jennings now?" Margaret wondered.

"Lord knows. With his snout in a bottle, I shouldn't wonder. I beg your pardon, my language is really becoming fit only for the stables."

"So should mine be if some brute of a groom allowed a horse to languish while he went on the toodle," she exclaimed hotly. "Well, let us see about the pitchfork first." As she spoke, she lifted a leather thong from a nail and took the pieces of the pitchfork from him. "Look to see how I do it," she commanded. "If it should break again you'll know what to do."

He watched attentively and admired the deft way in which Margaret worked. When she had done, he exclaimed, "Yes, I see now, and I can't thank you enough." He glanced skyward and added penitently, "It's getting late. I'm afraid I've kept you from your tea."

But Margaret had caught in his voice the longing of a hungry man. Impulsively she made a decision.

"I'm persuaded that two can work better than one," she said. "If you muck out the stable, I will tend to Beau." His protests were so outraged that she raised her eyebrows almost to the brim of her bonnet. "There's no need to get into such a pucker. I assure you that I know what I am about. Russkin was a perfect bear when it came to his horses. If I didn't come up to the mark, I was banished from the stable."

"But, hang it—I mean, dash it all," exclaimed Trent indignantly, "you shouldn't be hanging about the stable at all. It's not fitting for a lady. Besides, Beau won't let just anybody handle him. He's likely to roll his eyes and nip at you."

Margaret went up to Beau. Crooning softly, she ran her hand gently over the horse's face and rubbed behind his ears. With an almost idiotic expression of pleasure, the big gelding laid its head on Margaret's shoulder.

"You were saying?" She laughed.

Without further ado, she went to work on Beau's hurt foreleg. The horse, sensing that she knew what she was doing, stood still and allowed her ministrations.

"Now, then, my beauty," she half sang to him. "Well, sir, you are complete to a shade—the showiest of the lot. There, be easy. Don't you feel better already?"

A noise behind her made her turn her head.

She saw that Trent was working quite close to her, and she couldn't help noticing again that his coarse shirt and breeches were much too tight for him. They stretched across his broad-shouldered, narrow-hipped frame to delineate each line and sinew. Every movement emphasized the play of his muscles, and when he half turned in his labors, she glimpsed the hard line of his lean belly and powerful thighs and legs.

Being country bred, Margaret had seen men working before, yet now she felt disconcerted. Ken Trent exuded a virile masculinity that made the stable suddenly feel small and close.

Hastily she turned back to Beau, but her attention was no longer centered on the horse. *What* was Ken Trent doing mucking out Longmarsh's stable? she wondered. Why was a gentleman, and, if she did not miss her guess, a buck of the first stare, masquerading as the lowest of the low? Then it occurred to her that being a fashionable blade in London must cost money. Perhaps Ken Trent's creditors were after him.

If that were the case, his disguise was inspired. Not even the most persistent bloodhound would think of looking for a gentleman in a stable.

"Most ingenious," she murmured. "Really, very clever."

Trent paused in the act of pitching clean hay onto the stable floor. "What's that?"

"I was talking to Beau. Very intelligent he is, too, as are these gentlemen here." Margaret got to her feet, dusted off her skirts, and walked over to a pair of fine dappled grays. "Such small heads and broad chests and thighs. They're beautifully matched."

He nodded eagerly. "Hector and Ajax are like the ones I—" Trent stopped himself in time and added rather hastily, "But you mustn't waste any more time here, Miss Hannay. It's past sundown and your mother will be worried about you."

"She'll think that my employer has kept me past the time, that is all."

"She does that often, does she?" Trent asked. Feeling indignant on Margaret's behalf, he added, "Regular old griffin she must be."

"'Do or do without,'" Margaret quoted. Then she added briskly, "But you are right, it is getting late. I'll bid you good night, Mr. Trent."

"I'll walk you back to your cottage."

"That is really unnecessary," she protested. When he informed her that it would not do for a lady to walk unescorted in the dark, she smiled. "But it isn't even dark, and these are not the streets of London. Besides, I'm no fine lady."

For an answer he tossed the pitchfork into a corner and offered her his arm. She hesitated for an instant, then took it. "You didn't answer my question," he continued, as they began to walk. "*Is* it beastly being Lady Vere's companion?"

"Very," she said cheerfully, "but there are compensations. My lady does not insist I live at Vere Hall. I am allowed to go home each night to help my mother, which is a blessing since Mama's eyes are very poor. Also, on Wednesdays, which is today, I am given a half-day's holiday. Lady Vere reminds me twenty times an hour that other paid companions are not so fortunate."

"Need you continue with her? No, that's dashed impertinent of me," Trent amended hastily. "I'm sorry."

They had, by now, reached the other side of the woods. The day was settling into twilight, but this dimming did little to soften the outlines of the Hannays' cottage. The crumbling stone wall that girded the cottage looked decrepit in the half-light.

With her eyes on the scene before her, Margaret said, "I do need to work for Lady Vere or for someone like her. I fear that we are in what polite people call 'reduced circumstances.' My father followed the drum, you see. He was a captain in the dragoon guards."

"Was he?" Trent exclaimed. "That's a dashed fine regiment."

"Yes," she said with simple pride, "it is. And so was he. Very fine, indeed. But he was a fourth son with no expectations, and when my mother eloped with him against her family's wishes, they cast her out." She paused, remembering. "I knew the story from the time I was in leading strings, but I give you my word that I always thought being 'cast out' meant something good, not bad. We were so happy together in Shropshire on the small property my father bought when he sold out. Then he died, and our property was sold."

Intuiting that her quiet voice hid much pain, Trent held his peace.

"Mama came down with a fever, and it affected her heart and her eyes," Margaret continued. "She could not exert herself or see very well, and Papa's death made her even more fragile. I advertised myself as a governess, companion, anything that would permit us to live together." She paused to glance up at her companion. "What of you? Your position seems less tolerable than

23

mine. Being a lady's companion is bad enough, but having to be a groom—"

"It's because of Miss Jer—" That had slipped out before he could help it. Trent swallowed the rest of the name so that it came out garbled.

"Is Miss Jerre a lady in London?" Margaret asked.

Trent thought of a dozen explanations. Then he looked down into Margaret's frank eyes and knew he couldn't lie to her. Or, at least, he couldn't lie *too* much.

"She goes there for the Season. There are obstacles that keep us apart."

Margaret was mentally revising the scenario that had brought Ken Trent to Longmarsh. Not creditors, she told herself, but an affair of the heart. A duel, perhaps.

"I am so sorry," she said. "What is she like?"

Warmed by the sympathy in her voice, Trent enthused, "She is the kindest woman on earth. And the loveliest. She has beautiful golden hair and blue eyes and the most delicate white hands."

He looked down at his own hands as he spoke and frowned in disgust. He could hardly recognize these hands as his own. Newly formed calluses made ridges under his fingers, and grime had been imbedded into the palms. What would the fastidious Miss Jerryham think if she saw him like this?

Margaret read his thoughts. "Grandaunt Tab's soap will do the trick." He looked at her quizzically. "I'm persuaded that it would take the spots from a leopard. Mama used to make the stuff from a secret recipe handed down by Grandaunt Tab, who was supposed to be a witch."

"You're joking," Trent exclaimed, diverted. "A witch who made soap? But if your lady mother could spare a bar, I'd be grateful. I may have to work under Jennings, but I don't want to look like him."

Margaret agreed, but her mind had returned to an earlier topic. "Does Miss Jerre know you're here?"

Trent looked horrified. "Oh, good God, no. She'd never understand—I mean, she knows that we must be separated for some time."

He stopped talking as they reached the door of the cottage. Seen up close, the place looked more decrepit than ever. The walls of the cottage were leprous with age, and the roof sagged alarmingly.

"We're home!" Margaret exclaimed.

Trent was astonished that her voice actually glowed with pleasure. So did her face as she knocked on the door, then opened it, calling, "I'm sorry to be late, Mama."

From the unprepossessing look of the cottage, Trent had not expected to find so cheerful a room inside. A crackling fire exuded warmth, and there was a bowl of daffodils on the scrubbed wooden table. A few cheerful watercolors disguised the worst cracks in the rough plaster walls.

"I'm glad to see you, my dear, but who have you brought with you?"

The soft voice emanated from an armchair drawn close to the fire. On it reclined a diminutive lady in a black dress. Perhaps it was her size that made her seem so young, Trent thought. Or perhaps it was Mrs. Hannay's face, which was curiously unlined under masses of silver hair. Her smile was confiding and ingenuous, and her eyes were very like Margaret's.

"This is Mr. Ken Trent, Mama," Margaret was explaining. "He works at Longmarsh and has missed his tea because he insisted on escorting me home. I offered him some of ours—and a bar of Grandaunt Tab's soap."

Mrs. Hannay looked pleased and held out her hand, but Margaret laughed and said that the gentleman had better wash before shaking hands.

"And so should I. I have been playing with horses, Mama. Are you going to give me a scold?"

She tossed off her bonnet, ran a hand through her red-gold hair—long, lovely hair it was, Trent realized, now that it was not confined in that awful bonnet—and bent to kiss her mother's cheek. There was a note of loving teasing in her voice that recalled better days. Trent's heart lifted even as he protested that he could not impose on the ladies' hospitality.

Mrs. Hannay looked anxious. "We get so little company here, Mr. Trent. There is not much to tempt you, I am afraid, but I have cut bread and butter and there is some honey made here in the village. And there is a seed cake that Margaret made herself. It really is very good."

"I'm sure of it, Mrs. Hannay," Trent said gently. Some quality about the little lady made him feel protective of her, and the fact that both she and her daughter were so obviously sincere about wanting him to share their tea gave him the first real pleasure he'd had since he'd left

London. "I'd like it above all things," he went on frankly, "but first I must wash. I can't sit down in my dirt, ma'am."

He washed outside at the pump. It was the most ancient pump he had ever seen and threatened to fall apart in his hands. The pump, along with the cottage and the wall, invoked Trent's wrath, and with his usual forthrightness he told Margaret that Lady Vere should have made repairs long since.

Margaret was silent for a moment. "She apparently feels that this is good enough for us," she said.

He frowned but let the matter pass. Instead, he did his best to entertain the ladies over tea. It was no hard task. Once she had learned that Trent came from London, Mrs. Hannay plied him with so many questions that Margaret finally intervened.

"Mama, the poor man cannot even finish his tea," she protested.

Actually, this was far from the truth. Margaret was pleased to see that Trent had devoured several pieces of bread and butter and honey and was making severe inroads in her seed cake.

"No—give you my word—I'm enjoying myself excessively," he exclaimed, and watched the way Margaret's eyes danced when he told the story of Prinny trying unsuccessfully to squeeze his corpulent regalness into a too-tight coat. Trent, who had quite forgotten his position at Longmarsh, did not stop to think that the ladies might consider it odd that a groom should know such an *on-dit*.

Margaret did not think it at all strange, either.

By the time tea was over, she also had forgotten Trent's unusual occupation and was only jolted back to reality when he rose and said that he must return to work. Before he left he insisted on bringing in an armful of firewood, and on his return Margaret presented him with a large cake of oddly scented soap.

"You must scrub your hands into a lather," she explained. "The trick is in the suds, sir."

He thanked her. She was, he thought, a really excellent female and as game as a pebble. "I've never enjoyed tea more," he told her honestly.

She laughed. "A whisker if I ever heard one. Bread and butter and seed cake is hardly festive fare."

About to protest, Trent was suddenly reminded of a tea he had sat through at the Jerryhams a month or so ago. He thought of the liveried servants, the endless array of cakes and tarts and paper-thin sandwiches, and the ladies in their silks and jewels and their jealously attentive admirers. Most of all he thought of Miss Lavinia Jerryham, who had been a dream in a blue kerseymere gown embellished with Spanish sleeves. All that seemed a part of another world.

Seeing the faraway look in Trent's green eyes, Margaret guessed the direction of his thoughts.

"Heart up, Mr. Trent," she told him. "It will all come to rights. You have only to persevere."

He returned to the present with a jarring thump. Then, rallying, he smiled. "Thank you. And make sure you don't let Lady Vere bully you, Miss Hannay."

The light in her eyes dimmed a little, but she kept her smile. "No," she said stoutly. "I won't."

Chapter Three

"I must make her see reason somehow. Lady Vere cannot continue to keep me here."

Link, who was standing near the marble bust of Plato in the ground-floor anteroom, eyed Margaret worriedly, and she realized she'd been talking to herself. But, she reasoned, anyone who had been penned up with her ladyship for four days and nights was entitled to some eccentric behavior.

In spite of the fact that the weather had turned fine, Lady Vere had taken a chill. It was only a cold, but her ladyship acted as if she were on her deathbed. The doctor had been sent for five times, and the staff had been subjected to such harassment that the usually good-natured housekeeper, Mrs. Pollyshot, had snapped at Cook, who had become hysterical.

Such was her suffering that Lady Vere could not manage for an instant without her paid companion. She had commanded Margaret to spend her nights at Vere Hall, and Margaret had been forced to occupy the third-floor bedroom that had housed her ladyship's previous companions. It was a tiny room furnished with castoffs and redolent of camphor. It was also so close to Lady

Vere's suite that her handbell sounded like a cannon's roar.

Night and day that handbell had summoned Margaret, who had done her best to satisfy her employer's caprices. It was an impossible task, but she was used to that. What she could not bear was not being allowed to see her mother even for a moment.

Her request for an hour's visit to Mrs. Hannay had been coldly refused. How could Margaret be so unfeeling, so wanting in sensibility, Lady Vere had charged, as to wish to leave her when she was helpless? Margaret, thinking of her truly helpless mother, was beside herself.

Mama could walk a little, cut bread and butter it, but that was the extent of her powers. She could not see well enough, was not strong enough, to tend the fire or to cook for herself.

"I *must* talk to my lady today," Margaret fretted. Somehow, she must convince Lady Vere to return to the terms of their agreement.

A cough at her elbow broke into her thoughts and she saw that Link had come up the stairs to stand behind her. "If I might make so bold, miss," he began.

Murmuring "Yes, of course," Margaret tried to pay attention.

"I know you've been that worrit about Mrs. Hannay, miss. Now, seeing as my mam lives in the village a stone's throw from the cottage an' all, 'twould be nothing for her to put together a dish o' hasty mutton or such, and she says she could clean the place and make Mrs. Hannay all comfortable-like." Red in the face, Link concluded, "My mam said as she could start today if you wishes it, miss."

Margaret was relieved nearly to tears. Disregarding the fact that she couldn't afford to pay Mrs. Link for her services, she smiled blithely at the young man.

"That is so kind. Thank you *very* much. Please beg Mrs. Link to begin caring for my mother at once."

Link's cheeks went even redder at the warmth in Margaret's voice. A grin very nearly split his face in two.

"I am sure Mama will be glad for Mrs. Link's company as well," Margaret was adding, when Nancy, the chambermaid, tripped up, dropped a neat little curtsy, and informed Margaret that her ladyship wanted her in the morning room.

"And," she warned, "she's that ugly this morning, miss, as could curdle the cream in the jar, so be careful an' all."

Reddington was at this moment making his ponderous progress through the ground-floor corridor. He paused on the stairs to eavesdrop, and as Margaret hastened away, he heard Link exclaim, "What I'd like to know is why a fine lady like Miss Margaret has to put up with that old wi—"

"Link!" Reddington's snarl stopped the young man in midword.

Nancy started guiltily, and Link began to tremble at sight of their mutual tyrant.

A tall man with muscles gone to fat, the butler was a figure to inspire fear. He was regally dressed in the Vere livery, his scanty black hair was carefully pomaded, and his clean-shaven visage was set in awful sternness. His several chins, red as a turkey cock's wattles, quivered with outrage.

"I allow no disrespect from *my* staff, Link," Reddington hissed. "An underfootman and a mere chambermaid daring to criticize the quality? You should go down on your knees and give thanks that you do not lose your positions on the spot. Get on with your work this instant."

Link mumbled an apology. Nancy's black eyes snapped rebelliously, but she, too, dropped a knee. As they watched Reddington roll majestically past, she muttered, "That old bubble. His goose is pissed because he got a jaw-me-dead from my lady this morning. Poor Miss Margaret's going to catch it today an' no mistake."

But Margaret's heart was light. The thought of her mother being cared for by Mrs. Link was so uplifting that not even the gloom of Vere Hall depressed her. She was smiling as she passed the murky dining room and the cavernous great hall, and as she climbed the grand staircase to the second floor, she was humming. She skimmed past the long, dimly lit picture gallery and was nearly at the door of the morning room when she heard the sound of a crash.

An ominous silence followed. Margaret hesitated with her hand on the doorknob. Go on, you coward, she urged herself.

She knocked, then entered a room richly appointed with Louis XVI armchairs, Italian marble, and draperies made from Chinese silk. Several fine works of art hung on the walls and in the middle of the room was a carved cedar table bearing a collection of china figurines. Elsie, the young housemaid, was on her knees by this table frantically trying to gather up fragments of a Dresden shepherdess.

Automatically, Margaret moved to help. "Leave her," commanded Lady Vere.

Margaret's employer was by the window ensconced in a lattice-back Chippendale chair. She looked quite regal this morning, for her thick fair hair had been arranged modishly and her blue cambric day dress came from a Bond Street modiste. She had been accounted a beauty in her day, and her gray eyes, patrician nose, and rosebud mouth had been bait enough to catch Lord Vere and his considerable fortune. Even in her late fifties her ladyship retained an elegance of face and form, though her mouth was marred by its downward pull.

"I vow, I am sick of stupidity," Lady Vere was saying. "I do not," she added as a sob erupted from the kneeling housemaid, "wish to hear from *you*. I have stood your incompetence far too long."

Elsie sent Margaret a terrified look. "Oh, lor', mum, I didn't mean ter brush up agin' the table. I won't do it no more."

"Certainly you will not. You will leave Vere Hall today without a character. Now, get out of my sight."

Clutching fragments of porcelain to her chest, Elsie ran from the room.

As she pretended to right the remaining figurines on the table, Margaret spoke slowly. "Elsie Culp is the eldest of a large family, ma'am. I'm told that she has many younger sisters and brothers and that her mother is a widow who is dependent on her wages. I think—"

"You are not paid to think."

Lady Vere's pencil-thin brows had pulled to-gether—a familiar storm signal. Margaret knew that she should hold her tongue, but felt she had to add, "I collect that it was an accident."

"And *I* collect that it is I, not you, who pay the servants in this house." Lady Vere waved an imperious hand. "I am feeling more the thing this morning and will walk in the topiary garden. Instruct Palley to give you my cape and bring it here at once."

Margaret knew that by commanding her to fetch the cape, Lady Vere was reminding her that Margaret was little better than a servant. She forced herself to smile. "Of course, ma'am. Shall it be the velvet pelisse bordered with sable?"

Spiteful gray eyes narrowed. Lady Vere didn't care for Margaret Hannay's smile or her well-bred poise. She would have preferred fear, anger, or tears—reactions she'd come to expect from others under her thumb.

"If you weren't such an idiot, you'd know that was the one I meant," Milady snapped.

Margaret bit her tongue as she left the morning room. She clenched her hands at her sides and reminded herself, Do or do without.

"M-Miss Margaret?"

Elsie was huddled against the corridor wall. "If she lets me go without a character, I dunno know what'll become o' me," she moaned.

Forgetting her own problems, Margaret put an arm around the girl's narrow shoulders. "I did try to reason with her, but she wouldn't listen. I'm sorry."

Swabbing at her eyes, Elsie wailed, "I may as

well drown meself and be done. What good will I be to my mam an' all?"

Margaret wished there was something helpful to say.

"Will you talk to her again, please, miss?" Elsie begged. "Mayhap she'll listen to you."

It wasn't very likely, but as she looked into the upraised, tearful face, Margaret hadn't the heart to say so. "I'll do my best," she promised. "Wipe your eyes, Elsie, while I go get her ladyship's cape."

This took a long time. The dresser, Palley, took malicious satisfaction in making Margaret wait while she pretended to look for the cape. When Margaret returned to the morning room, Lady Vere was looking even more peevish.

"You took long enough," she complained. Disregarding her companion's apology, she snatched at the cape. There was the sound of cloth tearing.

"Dolt!" my lady screamed. "See what you have done!"

In snatching the cloak away from Margaret, she had torn one of the braided closures on the cape.

"It can easily be mended," Margaret pointed out. "Shall I—"

A stinging slap interrupted her. It had all the force of Lady Vere's arm behind it, and for a moment the blood sang in Margaret's ears. Her eyes flashed fire; her tongue itched to tell her employer what she thought of her. She almost opened her mouth to say those words.

Then Margaret remembered her mother. It had taken a long time to make a home out of the tumbledown cottage, but that had been accomplished. Now, with good food and rest, Mama was at last starting to regain her strength.

She couldn't lose her position now. With an effort that was actually physically painful, Margaret asked, "What do you wish me to do, ma'am?"

Noting the shake in the young woman's voice, Lady Vere smiled. "You are a clumsy fool," she lectured. "However, I suppose the ruined closure can be replaced. Go and purchase one immediately from the shop in the village."

Still struggling to hold her tongue, Margaret nodded.

"Don't just stand there rainbow-chasing," Lady Vere snapped.

But Margaret stayed where she was. "Before I do as you say, I must bring a matter to your ladyship's attention. Elsie is crying in the hall because she is persuaded that you actually will turn her off without a character. I told her that you spoke from anger and that I was sure that you would never punish a small fault so severely."

Lady Vere opened her mouth to give the minx a setdown she would never forget, but something in Margaret's face checked her. A sixth sense told her that if she dismissed Elsie, Margaret would also leave her employ.

No matter how objectionable the girl was, she did her work efficiently and without complaint and for a salary far below the ordinary. Besides, there was the principle of the thing: Lady Vere did not wish to let the Hannay girl go without first breaking her spirit.

Her ladyship forced her mouth into a smile that made her look more disagreeable than ever.

"I am served by fools," she protested. "I was merely giving Elsie a fright so that she would take better care from now on. I collect that she has learned her lesson."

"I'll tell her, ma'am."

Lady Vere sniffed. "Tell her on your own time. I have told *you* to go and buy me a new closure to replace the one you ruined. Why are you not already gone?"

Nancy was waiting in the ground-floor anteroom.

"Oh, Miss Margaret," the chambermaid breathed, "there's been a reg'lar dustup this time, ain't there? Elsie's been crying ever so, but we can't get her to tell us what happened wi' the mistress."

"No matter, it's over now." Margaret found it hard to speak normally. As she settled her bonnet on her head her hands were trembling, and she could see in the anteroom mirror the darkening mark of Lady Vere's slap.

"What happened, miss?" the chambermaid wanted to know.

"Elsie broke a figurine and my lady threatened to dismiss her. But Elsie is forgiven now and must return to work at once."

"But she's gone."

"Gone! Where?"

Nancy shook her head. "I dunno know. She just bursted out o' here. Wild-like, she looked."

Margaret remembered Elsie's words. "She spoke of drowning herself," she whispered. "Surely she could not have meant it?"

But Margaret knew what desperation could do,

and she remembered the look on Elsie's face. Ignoring Nancy's questions, she jerked open the side door and flew from the house.

Bunching her skirts in both hands, Margaret skimmed down the steps of the house, past the topiary garden, and down the path that led to the trout stream. Here she fairly tumbled down the bank.

At the water's edge she paused. The clear stream reflected sun and white clouds and her own anxious self. No drowned face stared up at her. Margaret began a sigh of relief, then realized that the housemaid's slight body could have floated downstream.

"Are you going fishing?" a puzzled voice asked.

She gave a startled cry and turned so quickly that she slipped on the wet grass. She would have fallen into the stream if Trent had not caught her by the arms and pulled her back. "Be careful!" he exclaimed. "What on earth are you doing here, Miss Hannay?"

She didn't waste time on explanations but turned back to the trout stream again. "You must help me look for Elsie."

His bewilderment faded as she explained, but he looked unconvinced. "The girl wouldn't drown herself just for being sacked," he protested.

"She was desperate."

"There's bound to be other positions," Trent pointed out.

"How could she get *any* position without a character?" Without thinking, Margaret grasped Trent's hand and began to drag him along with her. "She's the oldest child—her father is dead—and she feels responsible for her family." She glanced distractedly over her shoulder, begging, "Please help me find her."

The urgency in her voice reached him. "I'll go downstream, you go up," he said. Then he added, "But we won't find her, mark my words."

He was right. Half an hour's search ended without any result. "Where could she be?" Margaret was worried. "She must have walked farther on."

Trent felt this nonsense had gone far enough. "Don't be a pea-goose, Miss Hannay. Think. If you wanted to do away with yourself, would you walk miles before pitching yourself into the drink? No, you'd topple in right at the edge of the road, wouldn't you, and save yourself the trouble."

"That is the most heartless—" Margaret broke off, considering. "You may be right."

"Of course I'm right. There's no need to be hipped—er, worried. The miserable girl's probably at home and having it cheerful with her tea while we make cakes of ourselves."

A small chuckle escaped from Margaret. "That's better. Now, don't worry anymore but go and—hell and the devil—I beg your pardon, Miss Hannay—what's happened to your face?"

Margaret hastily turned away and made a great show of brushing mud from the hem of her dress. "I am afraid I walked into a door."

"I used that same excuse when I was six years old and my brother planted me a facer. It didn't fadge then, either." Trent slid a thumb under her reluctant chin and raised it to scowl down at the bruise on her cheek. "Did that old beldame do this to you?"

"It doesn't signify," she told him hastily. "What's important is that we find Elsie. If she's not back at Vere Hall soon, she *will* be dismissed without a character." She paused. "Perhaps she's gone home to Longmarsh-on-Hill. I'm to do an errand in the village, so I'll stop at Mrs. Culp's on the way."

Trent compressed his lips into a hard line. "I'll come with you."

"Don't you have duties to attend to?" she protested. "If Jennings finds that you've slipped off, you'll be in the suds."

He shrugged. "Jennings spends all his time devising new torments for me. He'll rake me over the coals no matter what I do."

As he spoke, a clamor from the near distance caught their attention. Looking up, Margaret saw several of Lady Vere's servants hurrying toward her.

"It's like watching a circus parade," Trent observed.

She frowned at his appreciative grin. That grin reminded her that though he might be playacting as a groom, Trent was a gentleman. No wonder he couldn't understand Elsie's desperation.

Margaret was a gentleman's daughter, but there was a world of difference between her and the handsome man beside her. No matter what had brought him to Longmarsh, Trent had obviously never walked the floors agonizing about expenses. And to worry about so lowly a creature as a servant would never occur to him.

Her voice had an edge to it as she said, "Those people are my friends."

Noting that this statement astonished him, she

went on deliberately. "The tall lad in the lead is Link, the underfootman. Next is Noah, the pot-boy, then Nancy, the chambermaid. The stout lady who is trying to keep up with everyone is the housekeeper, Mrs. Pollyshot."

Trent was speechless. Though not one of those toplofty mushrooms who considered domestics below his notice, he would never have dreamed of considering servants as friends. His own man, Weldon, would have collapsed at such a notion. But, Trent reminded himself, Margaret Hannay *was* a lady's companion. No doubt she dealt with servants on a different footing.

"I suppose they've come looking for, er, Elsie," Trent suggested.

Without answering, Margaret walked forward to greet the oncoming staff. Young Peter Link reached her first and cried, "Have you found Elsie, miss? Nancy told us what she'd said to you an' all and what you said to her—"

"I sort of put the puzzle together like," Nancy interrupted. "Has Elsie really drowned herself?"

"My brother's wife got drownded," the grimy pot-boy offered. "Fished 'er out of the drink, my brother did. Blue as anyfing she were."

Trent saw Margaret blanch and said tersely, "Be quiet, you little ghoul."

Link, who himself had been about to command the pot-boy's silence, stared suspiciously at the stranger.

"This is Mr.—" Margaret checked herself and amended, "This is Ken Trent. He's a—a groom at Longmarsh who has been kind enough to help me search for Elsie."

41

Her explanation was interrupted by the arrival of Mrs. Pollyshot.

In moments of deep stress, Mrs. Pollyshot was prone to forget the lessons she had taken in elocution. "I can't believe," she panted, "that that h'ungrateful girl would go and drown 'erself. After all us 'as done for 'er. It would be a terrible blot on the family if she'd done away wi' 'erself."

Trent said, "The silly girl's probably gone home."

"All the same—" Mrs. Pollyshot stopped talking and looked hard at Trent. It was obvious that both she and the other servants had noted the difference between his manner of speaking and his rough clothing.

"Now wot," the housekeeper muttered, "is going on 'ere?"

Margaret hastened to explain Trent's presence once more. "He was kind enough to offer to accompany me to the village," she added.

"We're coming along wi' you," Mrs. Pollyshot immediately said.

As they all straggled toward the village, Margaret overheard the pot-boy whisper that he was blowed if that there cove was a groom. She could not hear the underfootman's response, for Trent was speaking to her.

"You'll pass by the cottage on your way to the village. We can look in on Mrs. Hannay."

She looked yearningly in the direction of the cottage and all but wrung her hands. "I wish I had time. I have been obliged to stay day and night at Vere Hall, and I've been so worried about Mama. Mrs. Link is to go to her today, but—"

"No need to concern yourself, she's well." She looked at him inquiringly, and Trent admitted diffidently that he'd stopped by the cottage once or twice to see if Mrs. Hannay required any assistance.

"But how kind of you!" Margaret cried.

"No such thing, upon my word. I wanted to thank her for Grandaunt Tab's soap. That soap is a sovereign remedy for dirt." He hesitated before adding, "Besides, I'd wondered where you were, Miss Hannay. I'd not seen you coming home from Vere Hall these past evenings."

The thought that Trent was concerned for her well-being produced an odd sensation in Margaret. She felt somewhat confused as, aware of the listening ears behind her, she lowered her voice. "You need not have been anxious."

His voice turned grim. "But I *am* anxious. You must leave Lady Vere. Boxing your ears is the outside of enough."

She interrupted him. "You remember what Russkin said?"

"But surely—"

"Please don't concern yourself. Lady Vere and I rub along famously together. And do you know," she went on thoughtfully, "I believe that at heart she does not sitting to lose my services. That was why she allowed that Elsie might come back. I was able to do that much good, anyway."

Trent held his peace. The thought of an evil-minded old woman victimizing Margaret enraged him, but by now he had come to the somber understanding that Margaret had few options.

The first time he had gone to see Mrs. Hannay, the old lady had been sitting in the dark beside

43

a barely flickering fire. He had made it up for her, and she had been touchingly grateful. Before leaving, he'd made sure she had something to eat and that there was enough wood for the night, and after that he had come by at least once a day to see if all was well.

In the course of these visits, Trent had seen just how helpless Mrs. Hannay was. And that made Margaret helpless, too.

Trent scowled. If his wretched great-uncle had left him his money outright, he could have done a great deal for the Hannays. The devil of it was that, as a groom, he couldn't even help himself.

Exclamations from the servants now brought him to the realization that they had reached the village. Longmarsh-on-Hill housed the tenants of the late earl as well as independent sheepmen from the rich Cotswold country, and it was a prosperous place. Stone cottages, built of slate and cream-colored limestone, looked solid and respectable.

Even the small cottage near the end of the village had its charm. Roses were beginning to bud along the stone wall, and pale primroses grew among the greens planted by the house wall.

Link went to the door and tapped on it, and a woman with two children clinging to her skirts came to the door. She was worn and bent and looked more like the children's grandmother than their mother.

She bobbed a curtsy to Margaret and said, "You'll have come to talk to our Elsie, miss?"

Relief washed through Margaret. "Then she did come home, Mrs. Culp?"

When the woman nodded, Margaret gave her

the good news. Mrs. Culp ran inside to fetch Elsie, who began to cry again.

"It were you, miss, I know, as changed the mistress's mind. None else could a' done it," she wept.

Margaret cut short such thanks. "You must be a good girl and stop crying now. Make yourself ready to return with Mrs. Pollyshot and the others while I go to the shop for Lady Vere."

The housekeeper objected to this. It was not seemly that Miss Margaret should go shopping alone, like a servant. "Let Link go with you," she said, "or Nancy."

But Trent intervened. "I'll escort Miss Hannay to the shop and back to Vere Hall. All of you can go about your business."

He had spoken with the air of a man used to being obeyed, and Margaret saw the looks the servants exchanged among themselves. They said nothing aloud, but Mrs. Pollyshot later told Cook that she had been fair flummoxed.

"For obviously he was a gentleman to his boot tops," she exclaimed, "and never mind his clothes. Did I curtsy or did I not? That was the question. I didn't know what to do. Lawks-a-mercy, I was in such a state I nearly exploded."

Link's assessment was more succinct. "He's on the run," he muttered to himself as he watched Margaret and Trent walking away. "Running from the law or from Queer Street, he is, an' never mind his la-di-da airs."

Meanwhile, Margaret was expostulating with Trent. "There is no need for you to come with me. I am perfectly able to reach the shop unaided and return to Vere Hall."

"I know that. It's just that I want to take a closer look at Vere Hall. It's a specimen of, er, fine Tudor architecture."

Margaret didn't believe him, but she had to admit that she was glad of his company. It was Trent who insisted on stopping to see how Mrs. Hannay was doing, and the sight of her mother being cared for by the sturdy Mrs. Link eased Margaret's fears. She felt at peace when they left the cottage and could now enjoy the beautiful day and listen to Trent's account of Beau's healing leg.

But though Margaret seemed quite restored, Trent felt his concern increase as they neared Vere Hall. Eyeing the darkening bruise on her cheek, he said, "I wish that I could help somehow, Miss Hannay."

Margaret looked down at her skirts. "Can you remove mud?" she wondered.

He couldn't help grinning at her practical question. "It suits you."

Her eyes were almost golden in the sunlight, and when she smiled a dimple tugged at the corner of her mouth. "*Mud* suits me?"

With his eyes fixed on that dimple and the inviting curve of her lips, Trent shook his head. "Well, what I mean is that most ladies would be having fits because they'd got a bit of mud on their shoes. Not you. You're too sensible."

If she were sensible, Margaret thought ruefully, she'd be hurrying to return to her duties. Her ladyship would by now be beside herself.

He could read her thoughts, and in spite of his resolve to remain silent, he could not help bursting out, "Surely there are other positions!"

"No other mistress would allow me to spend my evenings with Mama. Besides—" Margaret broke off to groan, "Oh, Lord."

Trent followed the direction of her eyes and saw a group of people perambulating down the garden walk. First came Link, who held a parasol over a grandly dressed lady. Immediately following was a Friday-faced female in a dark coat. A liveried footman brought up the rear of the procession.

Margaret was saying, "If I hurry, I may . . . No, worse luck. She's seen me."

"She's seen us both," Trent amended. "So that is Lady Vere."

Margaret saw her companion's jaw harden. "Please," she pleaded, "don't antagonize her. Anything you might say will cause me grief afterward . . ."

She broke off as Lady Vere said, "There you are at last."

Trent watched Margaret's expression change as she made her curtsy.

"It took you long enough to make a paltry visit to the village. And, pray, who is your swain?" Lady Vere gibed. "Never tell me that the gape-seed attached himself to you along the way."

The muffin-faced virago behind my lady sniggered. Trent's cheeks blazed with heat. Several angry replies rose to his lips, but the pleading look in Margaret's eyes kept him silent. No doubt the old harpy would take whatever he said out on her companion.

"What's wrong, fellow? Lost your tongue?" Lady Vere jeered. "Faugh, you smell of the stables. Go back to whatever sty you came from. As for you, gel, your clothes are a disgrace."

Margaret glanced at Trent's wrathful face. So far he had held his tongue, but from the look of him, his restraint could not last much longer. "I'll change at once, ma'am," she said.

"You have been away from your duties too long. You," she snapped at Link, "give the parasol to Miss Hannay and go back to the house. She'll continue with us and enliven us with an account of how she met her barnyard swain."

Not meeting Trent's eyes, Margaret took the parasol from Link's hand and fell into step with the others.

Trent watched her go in a silence that lasted barely until the party was out of earshot. He then let loose with a stream of picturesque oaths.

Link came to stand beside him. "That's 'zactly how I feel about it," he said gloomily, "but you can't do nothing about it, no more can I."

Trent turned furiously to the underfootman. "The hell with that. Don't you work in the same house as she does?"

Link bristled. "If you thinks that someone like me has any say in anything ... But," he added hotly, "I tell you this. Miss Hannay's quality. Which is more than I can say for the mistress, an' never mind her title. All of us belowstairs, 'cepting the butler an' that vinegar-faced Palley, feels that way."

Trent remembered the shock he had felt when Margaret spoke of Lady Vere's servants as her friends. He felt a vague stirring of shame. He could see now that Margaret needed supporters in Lady Vere's stronghold.

After a moment he said, "I know that Miss Hannay's under your mistress's thumb, and there's not much you or I can do about it. But you are at Vere Hall and I'm not. If Miss Hannay is ever in trouble or in need of help, I want you to let me know."

Link's eyes had narrowed during this speech, and he appraised his companion carefully. He prided himself on being a downy one and as such could not be fooled by poor clothes. He'd thought that this well-spoken stranger, this gentry-mort wrapped up in groom's trappings, might be a Captain Sharp or a thatchgallows on the run. But now he did not think that this was the case.

No bad man could talk in that tone of voice about Miss Margaret, and no wrong 'un would look after her with such concern. Link now believed that under Ken Trent's rough shirt beat the true heart of a gentleman.

He looked with newfound respect at the hard-muscled, tall figure, at the resolute green eyes and strong chin. It wasn't his business to wonder at the doings of the quality, Link decided. It was not for him to ask why this gentleman was masquerading as a groom. It was enough to know that Miss Margaret had acquired a champion.

"Well?" A shade of impatience hardened Trent's voice. "You heard me, didn't you?"

"I heard you," Link agreed. "An' I'll let you know."

Chapter Four

Margaret desperately needed to scream.

She had wanted to vent her feelings all morning, and now the need to do so was almost past bearing.

It was Wednesday, her half-day. It was also the day during which she'd come within a hairbreadth of leaving Lady Vere's service. All morning the words that would have freed her had hovered on the tip of Margaret's tongue.

But she had not said them. She had smiled instead, and her employer had never guessed how close her companion had been to letting loose a bedlamite shriek.

She stopped walking and looked around her. Late April sunlight brightened the path that ran between Lady Vere's property and Longmarsh's estate. It dusted gold over daffodils and primroses, glinted through a copse of beech, and dappled the late earl's meadows where many sleepy-looking sheep were grazing. All was peaceful and serene. No one was in sight.

Margaret threw back her head and let loose a bloodcurdling yell. It felt so good that she tried it again. Then, carried away by the spirit of release, she tore her bonnet from her head and flung it into the air, aiming punches at it.

"Beastly, beastly woman," she cried. "I wish you in Jericho! You are a sour old bleater and so I tell you—"

A roar of male laughter stopped her in midsentence, and she turned hastily. A curricle, drawn by a pair of handsome dappled grays, had pulled up by the side of the road. Trent, grinning appreciatively, was leaning over the ribbons.

He clicked his tongue. "You wrong your beloved employer, Miss Hannay. I'd have added a few more choice epithets."

Her cheeks felt hot. "Do you make it a practice to creep up behind people?" she charged.

"Hector and Ajax don't *creep*. Is it our fault that you were yelling too loudly to hear us drive up?"

"I was not—"

"Oh, yes, you were," Trent assured her. "You were whooping like a savage. I've seldom heard anyone in better voice."

After a moment, she began to laugh. "You are right, I was having a tantrum. I know it was an idiotish performance, but it felt so good."

Trent, who was dismounting from the curricle, drew his dark brows together in a frown of concern. But all he said was, "Best way I know to raise low spirits is to go for a ride."

He patted the side of the curricle as he spoke. She looked doubtful. "Should you be driving the grays?" she wondered. "I collect that they belong to the new Earl of Longmarsh. He might object."

"He wouldn't," Trent said.

"How do you know?" she charged. "Have you ever met the man?"

"Have you?" he evaded.

With some asperity she exclaimed, "Now, why would a paid companion be presented to a man of such eminence? Lady Vere says that the title and estate have gone to the late earl's favorite great-nephew in London. I'm sure he would not like his grays to be driven about."

"Well, I'm a groom. It's my job to drive them," Trent reminded her. His eyes gleamed with challenge as he added, "But perhaps you're afraid I may go too fast."

Sunlight turned her hair to shimmering red-gold as she tossed back her head. "What fudge! I am not so hen-hearted as that."

"Well?" She hesitated, and he grinned enticingly. "I thought so. You're fighting shy."

Margaret gave up the fight. "Do your worst, sir. You'll see who's fighting shy."

As she spoke, she picked up her bonnet, and Trent asked in a pained voice, "For God's sake, you aren't going to wear that horror?"

She looked at the bonnet judiciously. "It really is quite shabby, isn't it?" Trent informed her that it would suit an old lady of ninety. "Lady Vere was sure that my other bonnet was much too frivolous for a paid companion, so I had to borrow Mama's. However," she added as she set the bonnet on her head, "I must wear it, or her ladyship will learn that I've been gadding about the countryside without proper covering."

The frown reappeared between his dark brows. "You should tell the old fiend to go to hell. Sorry, Miss Hannay. That just slipped out."

"Pray don't regard it. Such words are music to my ears." Margaret paused to stroke the horses before stepping up to the curricle. He handed her up, and she exclaimed, "Well, sir, I am prepared for anything."

"We'll see about that." As Trent set the grays in motion, Margaret couldn't help admiring the deft way in which he handled the ribbons. He had light hands and a precision of eye that made her certain that in his other life in London—the one he had left because of his duel over his Miss Jerre—he was an acclaimed whip.

"*Did* you meet him?" she wondered.

"Meet who?"

"The present Earl of Longmarsh. You did not give me an answer when I asked before. Are you acquainted with him?"

"I know a great many people in London," Trent hedged.

Margaret clapped her hands together. "So you *do* know him. Is he young, as Lady Vere said?"

"I suppose you could say so."

Margaret tilted her head to study his face. "From your tone I feel certain that you do not approve of him. Longmarsh must be some silly blood of the ton, a choice spirit who thinks it's hilarious to wear false whiskers and a false nose and to spend his time throwing waiters out of tavern windows." She nodded wisely as she added, "Oh, yes. I'll wager he kicks his heels at Vauxhall, too, and spends all his money in gaming hells."

Trent stared at her, astounded that a country-bred young lady should know about such goings-on. Before he could comment, she continued, "But never mind the kind of man young Longmarsh is, Lady Vere would dote on him. If his lordship ever appeared at Vere Hall, her ladyship would toadeat him in the most odious way. She worships titles. Now if you had a title, she would fall at your feet."

Trent hastily changed the subject and asked her what she thought of the grays.

"They are certainly a high-stepping pair," Margaret enthused. "Papa had a curricle, too, and he would take Mama for rides. She was in better health then. Later, he taught me to handle the ribbons."

"Did he, by Jupiter!" Trent brought the grays to a halt. "Let's see how you do."

She protested immediately. "How can I? It's been years and . . ."

"You've forgotten how," he suggested. Her brows puckered up, and he added insinuatingly, "Or else you've been telling me Banbury stories about your skill."

"Of course I have not. You are the most odious . . . You should know that I couldn't drive the new earl's curricle without his permission."

"Why worry about that spoiled slowtop? He won't mind."

Margaret hesitated. Trent held out the reins and shook them under her nose tantalizingly.

"It's open country," he murmured. "There's nobody about. You couldn't hit anything or overturn the curricle. What would it hurt to take a little spin?"

In spite of herself, she could not help taking the ribbons. The feel of them in her hands was irresistible and so was the look Trent gave her.

"Well, perhaps just a little way," Margaret murmured.

Trent leaned back and watched as she began to drive the curricle. At first she was stiff and apprehensive, but only a few moments had passed before she began to relax. Trent was surprised. He'd expected that she would be an adequate driver, but Margaret handled the ribbons as if she had been born with them in her fist.

He nodded approvingly as she took a neat turn in the winding country road. "All right and tight—I mean to say, you did that very well. You're quite a whip."

"High praise, sir." Her cheeks were pink with excitement, her eyes sparkled, and she held her head at a confident, almost jaunty angle. Even her tone and way of speaking was different. It was, Trent thought, as if a layer of frost had melted away from her.

"Now, what was that sigh about?" Margaret wanted to know.

"What sigh? It was a gasp of relief. I thought you didn't see that monstrous rock in the middle of the road, but you avoided it in the nick of time."

She shook her head. "You are telling me farradiddles again. Confess that you were thinking of Miss Jerre. Did you go riding together?"

With a guilty start, Trent realized that he had *not* been thinking of Miss Jerryham at all. He had actually been wishing that he'd met Margaret when Captain Hannay of the dragoon guards was still alive. He had been weaving a daydream in which he had just driven his curricle and matched pair up to the Hannay residence.

She misread his silence and said contritely, "Pray disregard the question. I have no patience with people who poke their noses in others' affairs."

To show her that he wasn't offended and also to atone for his own lapse into thought, Trent began to talk rapidly. "Naturally, Miss, er, Jerre and I went driving together in London," he said. "She's a fine horsewoman."

Margaret listened as Trent rhapsodized about how dashing his ladylove looked in her sky-blue riding dress and matching shako and was suddenly conscious of her own drab clothes. "She sounds like a nonpareil, Mr. Trent," she said cordially. "I hope I may meet her one day and wish you both happy."

Trent nodded. "But what of you? You, too, are a nonpareil. Did you ever drive your father's curricle in London?"

"Do you mean during the season?" Margaret smiled. "I'm a country girl, remember. Papa had no money to rent a London address, and besides, by the time I was of an age to make my come-out, Mama was quite ill." She shook her head as she added slowly, "How long ago that seems."

"Naturally you're long in the tooth now." Trent grinned.

"No, but I *am* one and twenty. I should be in my third season by now. And what a waste of money," she went on matter-of-factly, "for I'm persuaded that I would not have taken at all. No one would have wanted a country ragamuffin."

Trent said that he was sure that was not the case, but Margaret begged him not to be polite.

"I was once invited down to London with my parents," she explained, "to a rout that Lady Marshall was giving. Lord Marshall had been one of Papa's officers, you see. They were very kind and did their best to introduce us to members of the ton."

Margaret paused to add reflectively, "The ladies were very agreeable, but most of the gentlemen I met were odd. There were several red-faced bucks who drank too much and pinched the young girls on the sly, and the others were forever worrying about their clothes and the size of their buttons and the ways in which to torment their cravats." She shook her head in wonder. "Some young men actually had lead-whitened hands, and others had stained them brown. I remember that the backs of one man's hands were almost mahogany."

Trent glanced at his own hands. Thanks to Grandaunt Tab's soap, they were clean again, but his calluses had hardened and work in the sun had tanned them as dark as his face. He had never followed the vagaries of fashion or painted his face and hands, but several of his friends had. For instance, George Montesque liked to put on his breeches while they were still wet so that they would become skintight as they dried, and Button spent a fortune on coats and hats.

Thinking of his friends made him protest, "It's all harmless stuff. Besides, there are lots of good fellows in London who don't give a fig for dandying themselves up."

Margaret said pertly, "You mean the Corinthians, I collect? From what I overheard at Lord and Lady Marshall's, they thought of nothing but driving their curricles about, holding bouts at Cribb's parlor, and spending their time and money on the fashionable impures."

"Well, I like that!" Trent exclaimed, scandalized. "That's doing it too brown. You really oughtn't to know expressions like that. It's—it's not the thing."

Margaret tossed her head so vigorously that the ugly bonnet slid back to reveal her bright hair. "Fiddle. I learned many worse expressions, I assure you, from Russkin. Only, when I tried using them, he threatened to paddle me."

Trent grinned. Then he added, "What's that coming up ahead of us?"

The rolling pastureland through which they had been driving had given way to a village. It was larger than Longmarsh-on-Hill, though made up of the same stone houses and narrow village streets. The square tower of a Norman church rose behind a copse of young oak and beech.

"I collect that this village is called Harton-on-Wold," Margaret said. "It used to be a center for the wool trade in the Middle Ages and is famous for its church. Would you like to stop and look at it?"

On the verge of saying that this was the last thing he wished to do, Trent realized that he had never seen Margaret look so animated and interested.

"I'm fond of architecture," he said heroically. "Bring on your church, Miss Hannay."

She slowed the grays as they left the road and followed a narrow lane that led to the old church.

Margaret looked around her with interest. "I believe that the Romans built the wall you see along the way," she said. "Farther on there's an old barrow where the ancients buried their dead."

"How do you know all that?"

"Papa was interested in old England. He had many books about the history of the nation. When he died," she continued slowly, "I thought that what I had learned from him would enable me to become a governess. It would have been better, perhaps, but . . ."

She checked herself and made a great show of drawing up the horses. Trent, who had seen some of the brightness dim from her eyes, hastily asked what else she knew about Harton-on-Wold.

"Only that there's a new mineral spring nearby," Margaret said. "It was discovered by accident, I hear, and its fame has spread as far as London. Many fashionable people are coming here to drink the waters. Someday Harton-on-Wold may become as famous as Bath."

Trent was staring down the road. "There's an old fidget coming this way, probably the vicar." Rather hastily he added, "He'll take you round the church, naturally. I'll wait with the curricle."

"Oh, but that will never do. You are the one who loves architecture," Margaret pointed out wickedly.

The kindly old vicar looked mildly surprised when the shabbily dressed young man actually accompanied his mistress about the church. However, as Trent made no comment at all, the vicar soon forgot about him and addressed his commentary to Margaret alone.

This was perfectly agreeable to Trent. He followed in silence as the old gentleman rambled away, and not being the least interested in William Fitzwilliam, the founder of the church, or in the sainted Hubert, Bishop of Ortswick, who was interred under the altar, he spent the time watching Margaret's face.

She looked happier than he'd ever seen her, he thought. Happier, certainly, than when he'd seen her yelling in the meadow.

Damn and blast Lady Vere, Trent thought. I wonder what she's been up to?

After a long tour of the church, the vicar suggested that Margaret might wish to visit the churchyard. Querying Trent with a lift of her brow, Margaret agreed.

"The folk there will be quiet, anyway, and not go on nattering about Fitzwilliam and Hubert and Lord knows who else," Trent said gratefully when the vicar had ambled off. He held open the squeaking iron gate for Margaret, adding, "I've been meaning to ask you, why exactly was Lady Vere so abominable to you this morning?"

"Her ladyship is expecting guests and wishes to hold a ball in their honor. Do you have any idea what goes into planning such an assembly?"

"No, thank God."

"Lady Vere is determined that this will be no mere country hop. An orchestra is being hired for the occasion, and her ladyship is attempting to engage a very exclusive London caterer who is also a decorator. There has been an uproar," Margaret went on, "ever since the ball was an-

nounced this morning. First Lady Vere summoned the housekeeper, and poor Mrs. Pollyshot
nearly had spasms because of all the demands
placed on her. Then her ladyship saw Flood, the
chief gardener."

She dropped her voice to its lowest register and
mimicked, " 'Yer leddyship says I has to produce
flowers which is not in season—and that is *on*reasonable. I've been in service in this house, man
an' boy, fer forty-five year, but I'm not so old as
I can't look fer another post."

Margaret paused for breath, and Trent
growled, "And she blamed you for everything
that went wrong, I suppose."

"Naturally. She rang such peals over my head
today that I very nearly gave her my notice. But
then Link, who was standing by the door, sent
me such a droll look that I nearly burst out
laughing instead."

Margaret smoothed her hand over an old
gravestone as she spoke. That small hand shook
a little, as did her voice. Impulsively, Trent
reached out and covered her hand with his.

His touch steadied her, as did the wordless
sympathy of the firm, hard grip. Margaret's voice
was more her own as she continued, "Later, Cook
sent up a cup of tea. Nancy brought it and said,
'Lawks, miss, do not pay the mistress no mind.'
And little Elsie picked a rose and gave it to me
as I left. They are all so kind that I'm glad I
didn't give notice. Sometimes I can help them a
little in return."

She glanced up at Trent and saw the unhappy
expression in his eyes. The knowledge that he
wanted to help her, too, warmed her as much as

the hand that still lay over hers. She was suddenly seized by a need to lean into the comfort of his arms. The impulse was so strong that she could almost feel herself being hugged against the hard wall of his chest.

Shocked by the force of this idiotish notion, Margaret hastily drew her hand away. "I should not have told you my problems. I do not usually have such blue-devils."

Margaret's smile, Trent thought, was the kind with which brave men faced execution. He wished he could protect her and half lifted his arm as though to put it around her shoulders. Then he realized what he was doing and dropped it helplessly to his side.

Suddenly, inspiration came. "You're hungry!" he exclaimed. "Of course, that's it. Now, I saw a very tolerable tavern in that village we passed. What would you say to a ripping little tea?"

Her eyes sparkled. "I would say that I'd like it above all things. But," she added hastily, "what am I thinking of? It's late and Mama will be waiting for me, and Jennings—"

"Oh, hang Jennings. My real employer is the absent earl, and *he* won't mind." Trent threaded his arm through hers, adding, "Let's get away from these tombstones. Depressing things, I've always thought. Dead bores, in fact." She groaned but laughed, and he said, "That's more like it. Tea it is, Miss Hannay, and no arguments."

Not along afterward, they entered the common room of the Wool Pack Arms, where they were greeted cheerfully by the plump, bustling landlord. This individual was considerably surprised when Trent demanded a private parlor.

"Blowed if I know what their game is," he confided to his wife a few moments later. "The lady is very genteel, though down in the world, as you might say. But the man—dressed like a groom his nibs is, for all he acts like the lord o' the manor. Something very rum is going on."

His wife hurried off to peep at the interesting pair and came wheezing back.

"Old cabbage-head," she scolded her husband. "Anyone wi' one eye could see as they're lovers in disguise. Hiding from a wicked relation as wants her to make a miserable marriage, I shouldn't wonder." She sighed sentimentally. "Smell of April and May they do, and her so pretty and him so big and handsome wi' those speaking green eyes o' his. You give them anything they want, Jack. Serve up my best strawberry jam an' all."

Unaware of this discussion, Margaret helped Trent tackle the excellent tea served to them. Conversation was desultory for some time, but when the pile of currant buns and buttered crumpets, heaped with dollops of strawberry jam and clotted cream, diminished, talk began to flow again.

"I have not yet thanked you," Margaret said, "for all your kindnesses to us. Mrs. Link half believes that it is the little people who chopped the wood for us and mended the roof, but I know it was you."

Trent looked uncomfortable. "There's more to the local superstitions than meets the eye," he suggested hopefully.

Margaret ignored him. "Mama is sure that you are an angel in disguise sent to help us."

His cheeks reddened under their tan. "I'm grateful for Mrs. Hannay's good opinion, but, dash it, I haven't done anything."

"Moonshine, sir." When her eyes smiled like that, Trent thought with uncharacteristic lyricism, they reminded him of dewdrops glistening on autumn leaves. A curl had fallen forward and lay across her cheek like red-gold silk. Suddenly, he found himself wanting to brush it back and feel the satin-smoothness of her cheek under his fingertips.

Hastily, he put his hands in his pockets.

"Besides Mama, you have won yet another admirer," Margaret was saying. "I heard Peter Link telling Nancy that he's certain you are a lord in disguise."

Trent started.

"Your rank increases daily. You began as a mere baron but have since progressed to a viscount. Soon, I am persuaded, you will be handed an earldom."

Hastily, Trent begged her to remember that servants were gossips. "I had no idea *how* they talked until I sat down to table with them belowstairs. At the bottom of the confounded board, mind. My mother says that you don't know somebody till you've shared a meal with him, and she's right. A lot goes on that no employer would suspect."

Margaret agreed. "You can't fool servants. Now, Link believes that you are a gentleman who came to Longmarsh because of an affair of honor."

"An affair of . . . D'you mean a duel?" Trent asked, intrigued.

"Was it a duel?" Margaret whispered. Then she clapped her hands across her lips. "I didn't mean to ask that!"

Seeing how her hazel eyes still questioned him, Trent cudgeled his brains into action. "Duel? Ah, no. More like a rout."

"Between you and another of Miss Jerre's admirers?" she breathed.

"The Duke of Manfenny," Trent supplied glibly. "An odious young ninnyhammer. He couldn't hit the side of a barn at ten paces, but he called me out, so . . ."

"Did you . . . You didn't kill him?" Then, before Trent could reply, Margaret reached across the table and put a hand on his arm. "No, never mind," she said earnestly. "It's best that you don't tell me. Of course you came away because you didn't want scandal attached to Miss Jerre's name. You had to protect her."

"Naturally," he agreed.

"I didn't mean to rake up old hurts. I promise," she went on gravely, "not to breathe a word of this to anyone. And you have been wonderfully clever. No one would suspect a gentleman of disguising himself as a groom. It's quite unheard of."

Trent looked down at the small, white hand on his arm and felt like an out-and-out skirter. Lying went against the grain in any case, and falsehoods were doubly heinous when aimed at a right one like Margaret Hannay. The trouble was that the only alternative to spouting Banbury tales was to tell the truth.

As he paid for the tea and escorted Margaret past the bowing landlord, Trent warred with himself. He knew that Margaret Hannay was staunch as an English oak. She would never betray a confidence. And, though he had known her for so short a time, he regarded her as highly as the dearest of old friends, someone to whom he could tell his innermost secrets.

Should he tell Margaret about Longmarsh's will? Trent considered that his exile had been made even more unbearable because no one except the land steward, Howard Block, who had never so much as shown a shadow of himself, knew the truth about him.

Palchard had told him that he could disclose his identity in an emergency. He was sure that even his totty-headed great-uncle would rather have him come clean than to be constantly fibbing to a lady.

He came out of his thoughts to hear Margaret speaking in a troubled tone. "I did say I was sorry, you know."

She looked penitent and very lovely. Trent felt a sense of imbalance. He drew a breath to steady himself and took in some subtle flower scent she wore. Lavender or roses, he had no idea which, invaded his senses.

He felt a little light-headed as he began, "Miss Hannay, I have something I must tell you."

"Hi," somebody shouted. "Get out of my way, you bloody fool."

A curricle drawn by a brace of bays was bowling down the road. Trent had just enough time to catch Margaret by the shoulders and pull her out of harm's way. He had an impression of a well-cut greatcoat with many capes, spotless Hessians, and a disdainful red face under a beaver. Then he and Margaret were left standing in a cloud of dust.

"Damn you," Trent bellowed after the curricle. "Don't you look where you're going, you unspeakable jackass?"

"He did look," Margaret said.

She spoke in such a low, dispirited tone that Trent turned to stare at her. He blinked as he took in Margaret's drab gray dress and her hideous bonnet, then looked down at his rough clothes and workman's boots.

That arrogant dandy had looked and seen a groom and his wench—persons far below his notice. No wonder he had almost knocked them down.

"It is getting late," Margaret went on in that same, muted tone. "We had better go back."

Silently, they walked to the curricle. Margaret did not meet Trent's eyes as he handed her up. She wished that she could sink out of sight. Borrowed plumes, she thought miserably, don't make peacocks.

For a brief while she had forgotten who and what she was. For a happy hour or two she had felt like a lady again, delighting in a gentleman's company. But this was folly, and she knew it well now that her feet were planted in the real world again.

Do or do without, she reminded herself.

Then she glanced at her companion, and the misery in his eyes made her forget her own feelings.

Gently she said, "The tea was wonderful. Thank you, Mr. Trent, for a splendid day."

The words he'd meant to say earlier crowded onto Trent's tongue. He pushed them back.

He had several months yet to go before he might inherit his great-uncle's fortune of ten thousand a year. What could be gained by telling Margaret now, when he couldn't even protect her from a coxcomb on a country road?

Grimly, Trent snapped the reins and started the horses back along the way they had come.

Chapter Five

Trent's gloom clung to him long after he had left Margaret at her cottage and proceeded back to Longmarsh. He had never felt so down in the mouth. With Margaret at his side today, he had felt like himself again. Her pleasure in driving the curricle and the landlord's obsequious behavior at the inn had made him forget his humble position. Then that park-saunterer had nearly run them down, and reality had returned with a vengeance.

"He was driving a pair of commoners," Trent growled. "Those nags of his were short of bone and had no wind. And he dared to look at me as if *I* were below his touch. I should have dragged him from his seat and drawn his claret."

Until now he had not completely understood his degradation. Mucking out the stables, being ordered about by Jennings, eating with the servants—these things had been horrible enough, but he had managed to retain some sense of balance by reminding himself that in due time he would be lord and master at Longmarsh. But, in the meantime, to be looked at as a mere cockroach was more than flesh and blood could stand!

He had hardly served a month of his year's

sentence, and long days and nights of such humiliation stretched before him. "I should chuck the whole thing," Trent growled, but the thought of returning to London a failure shamed him. He could picture Monty's eyes popping. He could hear Button's disapproval.

And then there was Margaret. Trent thought of how she had ignored her own humiliation in order to try to make him feel better. He couldn't fight shy and leave her and Mrs. Hannay to Lady Vere's mercy.

"You stupid lump, what are you gawping at?"

Jennings was standing in front of the stable. His square face was florid with drink and his hamlike fists rested on his hips. "You're wanted at the manor," he growled.

Trent looked at the head groom with loathing. Ever since his arrival Jennings had done his best to make his assistant's life a torment. Being the sort who toadate members of the aristocracy while privately hating them, Jennings had been overjoyed to find a gentleman under his heel.

"Let 'im learn 'ow it feels to shovel manure," Trent had once overheard Jennings gloating to Ormsby, the junior footman at the house. " 'E won't like it, but 'e can't 'op it because 'e's on the run. 'E's either being dunned to death or 'e's killed someone and can't get 'isself out of the country. Oo'd look for a gentleman in a stable, eh?" And Jennings had smiled.

It had been a particularly nasty smile, a cousin to the one that now wreathed Jennings's thick lips.

"Took yer time, didn't you?" he demanded. "Or

mebbe you thought you was supposed to spend the 'ole day jauntering around?"

Several retorts rose to Trent's lips, but he merely pointed out that one of his duties was to exercise the horses.

"Don't yer be telling me about yer duties, you young fribble," the head groom snorted. "Get down to the manor, and be quick about it. The land steward's waiting fer you there. Don't keep yer betters waiting."

Trent wondered why Howard Block had finally decided to seek him out. Then it occurred to him that since the man knew his identity, there would be no need to pretend. It would be a short-lived respite, but being himself was something to look forward to.

He took pains to wash at the outside pump, then changed his shirt, combed his hair, and, in spite of Jennings's jeers, attempted to shine his boots. Finally, he strode down the path that led from the stable to Longmarsh Manor.

It was a long walk. As he approached the manor, Trent fancied that the fine old house, built of Cotswold stone that had weathered to a creamy gold, was sneering at him.

He shuddered, recalling his first sight of the manor house a month past. That day had been burned into his memory, and his first meal at the long servants' board belowstairs was an experience he would never forget. He had been seated so far down the board that such august personages as Gowan, the Scottish groom of chambers, and Mrs. Premice, the housekeeper, had hardly noticed him.

During that first meal Trent had been too sunk

in misery and fury at his great-uncle's treachery to do more than pick at his food. But in spite of his silence, the servants had marked him as different.

They had reacted to that difference according to their character. The red-headed cook called Trent "gallows bait" and sided with Jennings in making Trent's life miserable. The senior footman followed suit, but the younger footman, Ormsby, and the maids were friendly. The elderly housekeeper, reminded of her own grandsons, was kind. And from his Olympian heights Gowan unbent enough to be civil.

Trent was truly grateful for this civility, for he realized that the groom of chambers's word was law belowstairs. It was because of Gowan that Trent's detractors did not treat him worse than they did.

Today Gowan had sent Ormsby to wait for him at the servants' door. "Mr. Block's been waiting for over an hour," the young footman whispered. "Mr. Gowan's been in a taking acourse you wasn't to be found. Where was you?"

"I'm sorry," Trent said frankly. "I was exercising the horses, a task Jennings set me to do this morning. But I'm here now."

As Trent followed the junior footman, he looked about him. This was the first time he had been allowed into the sanctified upper realms of the great house. The manor had been built about the same time as Vere Hall, and possibly by the same architect, for there were the same depressing black oak beams and bare, wooden stairs. Trent caught a glimpse of a formal dining room, decorated with a forbidding table and stiff-backed

Jacobean chairs, then glanced at the high ceiling. Must be hell to heat, he thought.

Ormsby misinterpreted his silence. "Don't you worry," he whispered. "Mr. Blount's not knaggy nor mean-like. And I 'eard Mr. Gowan tell Mrs. Premice that it were a shame that Jennings treats you as 'e does. Nobody likes that Jennings, and that's a fact." He hesitated, then added, "There's tea in the kitchen, and Cook ain't around. Come and 'ave a cuppa later, when yer done."

The footman's kindness warmed Trent. There were good people at Longmarsh, he thought. And the house could be made more comfortable. Trent eyed a hideous armoire that stood in the hallway and thought that if he lasted long enough to assume control, his first act would be to pitch out most of the furniture.

"Shut the door behind you." The command came from a balding individual attired in a natty dark grey superfine, a somber cravat, and a black waistcoat. This elderly personage was seated behind a large desk, but when Trent complied with his command, he jumped from his chair and approached Trent deferentially. "How do you do, my lord?" he asked.

Mechanically, Trent held out his hand and felt it being shaken.

"I beg to present myself, Howard Block is my name," the land agent went on. "I served his lordship, your great-uncle, for thirty years. I hope that my service may please you also, sir."

The contrast between Jennings's abuse and this civility was too much. Trent barely managed to nod.

"I should, of course, have waited on your convenience, but your great-uncle's will stated that no one here at Longmarsh was to know your, ah, identity save myself." He chuckled and raised a waggish finger. "Of course, there are suspicions. Yes, indeed, there are. You can't make a silk purse into a sow's ear, eh, sir? The servants' gossip is that you have escaped from some, ah, crime and are in hiding."

Trent nodded gloomily. "Jennings believes it, certainly."

"From this moment," the land agent intoned, "Jennings has ceased to matter. You will take up new duties, sir, as my assistant. You have been, ah, promoted, as it were."

Trent stared. Block bowed. "It is *infra dig*, of course. But you could not be raised higher without arousing suspicions."

Trent sank down into a chair and surveyed Block with intent green eyes. "Let me understand this. I no longer work for Jennings?" Block bowed assent. "But won't 'suspicions' be raised if you take me as your assistant? The servants will talk."

"With a few exceptions, sir—of whom you are no doubt aware by now—your future staff is sympathetic and will delight at your good fortune. They will agree that a man of your quality is much better suited to be my, ah, assistant than, shall we say, mucking out the stables."

"Then why—"

Block interrupted again. "Permit me to say, sir, that the late earl was an original thinker. He felt that a man could not enjoy the mountain peak until he had scaled it from its foot. But you have done enough, ah, scaling, and besides, his lordship felt that learning about your estate would be beneficial to you when you reveal yourself as the Earl of Longmarsh."

When he revealed himself. The magic words echoed in Trent's mind as the land steward proceeded to explain that his living conditions would be changed immediately.

"I collect that you now lodge in the small room in the back of the stables? As my, ah, assistant, you will be put up at the cottage near the woods that border the estate. A woman from the village will come daily to cook and clean for you."

Block extracted a key and placed it on the table. "Naturally, my lord, you will need to change your wardrobe. May I recommend my tailor to you? His cut will not be of the quality *you* are accustomed to," he went on unctuously. "But you cannot show yourself in coats made by Scott yet. Also, you will require transportation. Pray choose a horse that suits you from the stable."

Trent felt a little breathless. "You seem to have planned things to the last detail," he exclaimed.

He recalled his earlier gloom, his longing to escape to London. That seemed so foolish now. And Block was right. He had learned a great deal about his staff, and that knowledge would serve him in the future. Perhaps, Trent conceded, his great-uncle was not quite the birdwit he had appeared to be.

The spring was back in Trent's step as he got to his feet. "Lead the way to this cottage, Mr. Block. That is," he added with relish, "as soon as I pay a visit to the stable. I wouldn't miss seeing the look on Jennings's face when he sees me commandeering Beau. Not for a hatful of guineas."

Good news needs to be shared in order to be savored, but as much as he wanted to tell Margaret of his good fortune, Trent was much too busy to do so. Moving to the comfortable cottage at the edge of the woods took some time, and it was immediately apparent that being an assistant land agent was no sinecure. Learning the tenants' names, acquainting himself with their families, resolving their problems, and making the rounds of a productive estate occupied each waking moment.

It was a week before he had the time to seek out the Hannays, and as he strode through the woods in the early twilight, Trent wondered if Margaret would be at home. He was half afraid that Lady Vere had detained her past her time, but his heart lifted when he heard the screescraw of the old pump.

Margaret was struggling with it. "Here," Trent called, "let me do that."

She looked over her shoulder, and her smile was as bright as a sunrise, but she didn't stop pumping.

"You couldn't. There's a knack to managing this stubborn old fidget. What, sir, will you?" she demanded in mock wrath as the water gurgled and went dry. "Take that, sir. And that."

Water started to gush again. Watching her with an appreciative grin, Trent suddenly recalled the one time he had seen Lavinia gardening. She had been wearing a day dress of sprigged blue muslin, and a pale blue ribbon had curled saucily about the brim of her sun hat. Her abigail had carried her watering can and gardening shears.

By contrast, Margaret was dressed in a simple green cotton dress. It was cut high at the waist and was unadorned except for a ruching of old lace at the throat. But against that creamy lace Margaret's hair shone like fiery silk, and her cheeks glowed from her exertions. Trent had never before seen such a vivid face.

"There," she panted at last. "This is enough water for now. Mama will be so glad to see you. Will you have time to take tea with us?"

"Only if you let me carry the bucket." As he took it from her, Trent added cordially, "You're looking famous, Miss Hannay. Is Lady Vere giving you less trouble?"

He hadn't realized how much he missed her chuckle. "No, alas. Perhaps I have become inured. Or simply numb."

He frowned, and Margaret had the inexplicable wish to smooth his knotted brow. She clasped her rebellious hands behind her back and said heartily, "I must not deprive Mama of seeing you for another moment. Come in, Mr. Trent."

Mrs. Hannay welcomed Trent with delight. Margaret watched her mother's pale face turn rosy as he shook her hand and thought that the lifting of her own heart came from this source. Mama had missed Trent and had often remarked on his absence.

Mrs. Link had gone for the day, so Trent insisted on helping Margaret set the table for tea. He then escorted Mrs. Hannay to her seat as if she were a duchess. But instead of taking his own chair, he remained standing and cleared his throat.

"I've got some news."

He's heard from Miss Jerre. The thought touched Margaret's mind and left an unexpected chill. Widgeon, she then rallied herself, why shouldn't he hear from his ladylove?

"You are being very mysterious," she charged. "From your face, I collect that it is *good* news."

When he had told them, Mrs. Hannay clapped her frail hands. "That is excellent," she cried. "I had fretted so about your being forced to work in that odious stable, but assisting Mr. Block is something that a gentleman may do very well. Do you not think so, dearest?"

"Yes, indeed," Margaret agreed. It seemed as though she couldn't stop smiling, and the frank happiness in Trent's eyes lightened her heart. "So, you are going to be a man of importance. You will ride about on Beau in a toplofty way or sit smugly in Mr. Block's landaulet." Her nose in the air, she pantomimed Trent's progress and added roguishly, "Naturally, we poor peasants will be quite below your touch."

Mrs. Hannay clicked her tongue and said that Margaret was being impertinent, but Trent laughed. When he thought of how subdued their last parting had been, he was glad to see how her eyes sparkled with mischief.

"Be careful," he warned, "or I might find you trespassing on Longmarsh land and make you pay the consequences."

He had said it to make her laugh, and she did.

The clear sound of that laughter made him think of a friendly fire found unexpectedly in winter.

"Now," Mrs. Hannay reproved, though her own eyes twinkled, "you must not talk so foolishly, you children. Have your tea, Kenneth." She stopped to add apologetically, "I beg your pardon for addressing you so, but you put me in mind of my own brother when he was your age. I hope you do not mind?"

Assured that Trent not only did not mind but liked it above all things, the old lady looked pleased.

"In that case," she said, "I know you will not think me forward. Margaret dearest, will you fetch my knitting? This," she added when her old-fashioned knitting bag had been brought, "is something against the chill nights. I thought to knit a scarf for you since you labored in that horrid stable, but now you can wear it as you drive about your business."

Margaret watched Trent as he took the scarf. Pleasure, gratitude, and a strange humility washed over his fine features, and the look in his green eyes was gentle as he knotted the scarf around his throat.

"Ma'am, this is really too good of you. I'll wear it proudly."

He took Mrs. Hannay's hand and kissed it. Margaret, watching, noted that there was less practice and much more heart in the way Trent bent over the old lady's hand.

Mrs. Hannay's eyes had filled with tears, and Margaret was moved, too. But she smiled and said, "I vow, Mama, that he is like a knight with his lady's favor."

Unaccustomed to the emotions that were making it hard for him to swallow, Trent was only too glad to follow Margaret's lead. "And so I am. Bring on the dragons, fair damsel—Sir Trent to the rescue."

"Best to postpone your rescuing till after your tea," Margaret suggested, and Mrs. Hannay said that Margaret should heed her own advice.

"It has been more difficult than usual for my daughter," she added earnestly to Trent, "during these last few days. Preparations for Lady Vere's house party and ball are causing so much confusion."

Margaret made light of her troubles. "We mark the days in crises," she joked. "Today was the Crisis of the Musicians. Indeed, it was like watching a play." Swiftly, she painted the scene: my lady enthroned in a straight-backed Jacobean chair in the sitting room with the fawning musicians arranged before her.

"Lady Vere ordered the musicians to play something to show their skill, so they began a waltz. In the midst of it, we heard a crash in the ground-floor anteroom. Link had been dancing a jig with Nancy, and they had upset that horrid bust of Plato."

Trent burst out laughing. "What did Lady Vere say?"

"The wonder is what Reddington said. When Lady Vere demanded to know the reason for the noise, he explained in his most repressive tone that the side door had been open and had blown shut. What he said to Nancy and Link, I shudder to think, but they looked most subdued when I saw them later."

"So the musicians have been hired. And the caterer?" Mrs. Hannay inquired.

"Lady Vere is triumphant that she has managed to secure Barnaby of London."

Trent looked surprised. "A coup, I'd say. Barnaby's quite in demand. Monty—a friend of mine—tried to engage him for his sister's come-out and couldn't."

"Lady Vere was anxious to have him because he is supposedly related to Sir Stephen Barnaby of Eastwick. Also, he is no mere caterer but is reputed to be a master decorator who can transform any house into a palace."

Trent observed that transforming Vere Hall would take a miracle, and Margaret agreed.

"Barnaby says he can do it, but that remains to be seen. He came to Vere Hall yesterday with his minions and outlorded everyone, even Reddington." Margaret pulled her mouth into a downward curve, narrowed her eyes, jerked up her chin, and drawled, " 'If your leddyship wishes *meh* to oversee the catering of the ball and the decorating of your residence, *Ah* must hev *carte blanche.*' "

"He sounds like a counter-jumping mushroom. What did Lady Vere say?"

"She agreed to do anything he wished. She wants to make an impression on her guests. I told you she adores titles, and the ball will be full of lords and ladies and colonels as well as the local gentry."

The conversation now turned to Trent's new duties, and he began to talk about Longmarsh's tenants and their problems. The most bothersome problem at hand, he told the ladies, was

Wickwell's youngest son, who was ailing with fever and a bad cough. The ladies listened with great concern, and Mrs. Hannay suggested several different remedies.

While he listened to the old lady, Trent's eyes strayed to Margaret. In spite of her smile, he now saw that she looked tired and that there were faint shadows under her eyes. That evil harridan, he fumed, but Margaret was in truth feeling happier than she had all week.

When she had not seen Trent for so many days, she had been sure that he had gone back to London. Though she had told herself that he owed her no good-byes and certainly no explanations, she had felt an inexplicable sense of loss. The days with Lady Vere had seemed longer and more tedious. Margaret had felt exhausted and uncharacteristically close to tears.

Tonight, when she had seen Trent at the well, her heart had leaped with pleasure. And he was pleased to be with them, too. Margaret watched laughter soften the hard planes of Trent's face, and the thought that had been in her mind ever since he had given them his good news solidified into resolve.

I'll do it, she told herself.

Later, when Trent at last rose to go, she accompanied him outside and walked with him past the tumbledown stone wall that bordered the cottage and out onto the path toward the woods.

"You have Mama's gift?" she asked him as they came to a standstill near the gate.

He patted his pocket. "How did she manage to make this? The poor woman can scarcely see."

"Mama was gifted with her needle before her

eyesight began to fail, and she can still knit a little." She began to say more, then broke off feeling suddenly shy and undecided.

"What is it, Margaret?"

In his concern, Trent didn't realize he had used her given name. She did. Her eyes flew up to meet his, and she saw that he was looking down at her with an expression that she could not define.

Margaret drew a deep breath and found her lungs invaded by the fragrance of spring and Trent's clean, distinctive scent. It was with an effort that she managed to speak in her usual, cheerful way.

"I have a gift for you, too. It is . . . well, by way of celebrating your rise in the world." She held out a book, which he took somewhat doubtfully.

"A gift for me?"

Her heart fell at his expression. "It—it's about old English buildings," she stammered. "It's really a gooseish idea, but you said you were interested in Tudor architecture, even though I know you were only funning."

He was silent for a moment before asking, "It was your father's book, wasn't it?" When she nodded, she heard his voice soften to a tone she had never heard him use before. "This is the finest, the most precious gift I've ever received. I'll treasure it."

Trent knew that the gift had come from Margaret's heart. She was looking up at him, her mouth soft, her eyes tender, and suddenly the air around them seemed charged and close, as though a thunderstorm were about to break.

Trent started to say something and found he couldn't think of anything but her name.

"Margaret . . ."

She gave a little sound that was something between a gasp and a sigh and walked blindly forward into his arms.

As their lips met, Margaret felt almost weightless. It was as if she had been lifted off the earth. Trent's lips, cool and sweet and sure, echoed the message she had seen in his eyes. A nagging voice somewhere in her brain begged her to reflect that what she was doing was unwise, but her senses, thrilling to a more exciting music, had no trouble drowning out that voice.

But the wretched voice of her common sense would not go away. "Listen, you gudgeon," it whined. "Don't you have any pride? Remember Miss Jerre."

Miss Jerre.

For the second time that day, and with even more force, the name seared across Margaret's mind. It reminded her that the man who was kissing her was madly in love with a London beauty.

Trent felt his hitherto willing partner go suddenly stiff within the circle of his arms. For a moment he held her more tightly, and then a cold wind seemed to blow across his senses. Bedazzled for a few moments, he had forgotten that such a place as the outside world existed, but now reality stared him in the face. He, the worshipper of beautiful Lavinia Jerryham, was kissing another woman.

Not another woman, Trent protested silently. I'm kissing Margaret.

Then he realized what he'd done—what he was doing. His arms loosened around her, and he stepped back so quickly that he stumbled. They looked at each other with wide, troubled eyes. Margaret's lips parted, but no words came out.

Trent cleared his throat. "Miss Hannay, I—"

"Please don't," she begged.

"Don't what?"

"I collect that you are going to say something commonsensical and tedious, such as you kissed me only because you were overwhelmed by my gift."

It had been precisely the excuse that Trent had been about to offer, but now he demanded, "What gave you that notion?"

"Well, what were you going to say?" she charged. Her voice was like a caress, Trent thought, and there was such a *look* in her eyes. Her lips had never seemed more inviting. "What?" she challenged softly.

Trent couldn't help himself. He leaned forward toward her just as she leaned toward him. As though they had a mind of their own, his arms reached out to gather her to him once again.

"I say, are you sure this is the way to Longmarsh?"

The plaintive question came from the direction of the woods. Trent and Margaret sprang apart as two men on horseback came trotting toward them through the twilight.

Trent immediately put Margaret behind him, saying tersely, "Go back to the house, Miss Hannay. They may be cutpurses. Or highwaymen."

"Fudge," she replied scornfully. "They are nothing of the kind. Just look at them."

Trent strained his eyes in the half-light. One of the men was tall and sat his respectable bay in a disinterested way. His companion was short and rotund and gave every evidence of being vastly uncomfortable in the saddle.

"Good Lord," Trent exclaimed, "they look like Button and Monty."

The tall, languid figure started. The short, pudgy one almost rolled off his horse. "Trent?" he gasped.

"It *is* you." Momentarily forgetting Margaret, Trent strode toward his friends. "What brings the two of you to Longmarsh?"

George Montesque, who was attempting to make himself secure in the saddle, uttered a faint groan and said, "Hunting."

"What, you?" Trent grinned. "Gammon. You abominate riding to hounds. What did you really come here for, Button?"

The languid horseman put up a quizzing glass, let it fall, and drawled, "But really, dear fellow, it's *why* we are here that is at issue. We are hunting with Lord Korrowin, don't you know. He was good enough to invite us to Norsby, which is nearby. Isn't that right, Monty?"

Montesque agreed that that was exactly what had happened.

"You both came up here to hunt with Korrowin? Stubble it," Trent exclaimed scornfully. "You think Korrowin's a totty-headed nincompoop, Button, and if I remember correctly, Lady Korrowin has set her cap for you. She's got a daughter, doesn't she?"

Margaret, torn between embarrassment and laughter, watched the languid horsemen jerk upright. "I beg you will not mention the matter, Trent," he implored in an agitated tone. "Miss Adela Lakehart is an antidote who would cause a man to fly to the Americans if she but looked at him a second time." He shuddered and then added, "You wrong us. We told Korrowin that we came to hunt with him, but, don't you know, we have other business at hand."

He broke off, coughed, and looked significantly at Margaret, and Trent hastily made introductions.

"Miss Hannay, I beg to present my friends from London," he said formally. "The Honorable George Montesque, Mr. Jermyn Butterworth. Gentleman, I give you Miss Hannay."

It was not so much the introduction as the tone in which it was uttered that caused Montesque (as he said later) to prick up his ears. "Miss Hannay," he wheezed, gallantly attempting to bow. "Your very obedient. Beg you'll forgive the intrusion. Fact is, came looking for Trent. Didn't know he was, ah, engaged."

"I pray you will not regard me," Margaret protested. She turned to Trent and held out a hand, saying, "I am very glad you came to tea, Mr. Trent. Good night. No, truly, it is not necessary to escort me home. It is but a step."

He shook her small, capable hand and, with a feeling of uncharacteristic befuddlement, watched her step briskly down the path.

His attention wandered until Montesque said plaintively, "Got to get down. Always could think better on my own feet. Oh, hold still, you miserable brute."

Trent saw that his friend was attempting to

dismount. He held Monty's horse for him while wondering what had possessed him to be so cockle-brained as to come out riding at this time of evening.

"You could have found me in daylight," he added. "It would have been easier if you could see where you were going."

Montesque and Button exchanged glances. "Well, that might have made it awkward," Button said.

"Gentleman don't consort with mere grooms, is that it?"

Heedless of the edge to his friend's tone, Montesque nodded. " 'Struth, Trent. Way of the world. Proper cakes we'd have looked, riding up to the stables and asking for you!"

"We might have given the game away," Button added more diplomatically. He paused. "That person you were with just now . . ."

"Miss Hannay," Trent said shortly.

"Seemed to me to be a lady," Button observed. Trent assured him, even more curtly, that she was exactly that. "In that case, you do her a great wrong, Trent," Button reproved. "Is she a governess?"

There was an ominous note in Trent's voice as he explained. Button shook his head in languid disapproval. "A lady's companion and a groom—unheard of."

Trent requested his friend not to talk such slum. "I'm not really a groom, as you well know. And Miss Hannay's a lady."

Again, Montesque and Button exchanged glances. "Delicate matter, dear boy." Montesque sighed. He stepped forward and patted Trent's arm. "Very delicate. Beg you'll remember our friendship when I say it's wrong of you, Trent. Shouldn't trifle with a lady. Mean to say, you being the Earl of Longmarsh and all that, and never mind about the money for the moment. Ain't ton at all to dangle after a lady's companion."

"Monty," said Trent in a deadly calm voice, "if you don't stop patting me, I will plant you a facer. I am not trifling with Miss Hannay. She's like a—a—"

"Sister?" Button suggested doubtfully.

"Well, no," Trent admitted, somewhat taken aback. "Though I hold Miss Hannay in as high a regard as I would regard a sister. She's a—a valued friend."

"Ah," Montesque murmured.

"I don't like the tone of that 'ah.' I said a friend, and I meant it. I did not mean a *belle amie*."

Button intervened. "We didn't travel ninety miles from London to brangle with you, dear fellow. We used Korrowin and the hunt as a blind, don't you know. It was the only thing we could think of on short notice, and, believe me, it entailed sacrifices that go beyond the mere bonds of friendship. You are quite right about Monty's aversion to hunting, and as for me, the prospect of being pursued by Miss Lakehart is beyond the edge of enough. No. We are here for your own good."

There was a pause. "Here to bring you news," Montesque added portentously.

"Well, let's have it," demanded Trent. "What are you being so damned mysterious about?"

Button nodded to Montesque who drew himself to his full height. He attempted to suck in his stomach as he announced dramatically, "Miss Jerryham is coming to visit Lady Vere. She and her mother will arrive at Vere Hall next week."

Chapter Six

"*Miss* Jerryham coming *here*!"

Trent's exclamation was so loud that it startled a bird that had been dozing on a nearby branch. As the bird took squawking flight, Trent seized Montesque by the wide lapels of his riding coat and lifted him several inches off the ground. "Monty, if you're bamming me . . ."

"Give you my word I'm not," Montesque choked.

Button commented, in a bored way, that if Trent thought that they had come all this way for a joke, he was touched in his upper works. "So you'd better stop ruining Monty's coat," he added.

Trent flushed, apologized, and lowered his plump friend to the ground. Then, in his torturously slow fashion, Button explained that Miss Lavinia was making the journey with her mother in order to visit Lady Vere. "Salad-day friends, don't you know. Lady J. and Lady Vere, I mean, not her daughter. Thought you'd want to know, old fellow," he added kindly.

"But it's the middle of the Season," stammered the bewildered Trent, "and Vere Hall is a curst dull place. No girl in her right mind would want to go there."

"It's the new mineral spring in the area," Button said. "Lady Vere wrote to Lady J. about it, I suppose, and Lady J. wants to sample the waters, something I can't understand since mineral water is hideous stuff. Vile, in fact. I wouldn't wish to inflict it on a dying man. All the same, Lady J.'s hipped on that sort of thing, and besides, there's that other thing, isn't there, Monty?"

Montesque, who was smoothing the lapels of his coat, replied sulkily that it was probably all a hum.

"What's a hum? Look, Monty, I'm sorry about your coat, but if you don't tell me what's happening, I'll be forced to grab hold of you again. I can't help myself."

Montesque hastily retreated a few steps. "Heard it from Upton," he explained. "Lady J. don't like the way young Beresford's been languishing after her daughter."

Trent gave a shout of laughter. "Do you mean to stand there and tell me that that young ninnyhammer's been dangling after Miss Jerryham? It's got to be a hum, George. Lady J. wouldn't worry about Beresford. No one would take him seriously."

"You don't know the half of it," Montesque said. "Young nincompoop's been laying a siege on Miss Jerryham since her arrival in London. Got a Gypsy band to serenade her one evening. Sends her mountains of flowers. Lies in wait for her at the park. Ogles her when he sees her. Overdoes it, Trent, give you my word. Very bad ton. Makes Miss Jerryham appear ridiculous—

and that discourages eligibles. And that ain't the worst of it. He stands outside the house and carries on."

Trent frowned. "What do you mean, 'carries on'?"

"Appears at two in the morning and hangs about till dawn, staring at Miss Jerryham's window. Lady J. threatened to call the watch. Give you my word. Apparently her butler's sick of seeing Beresford's silly face first thing in the morning. He might give notice."

"I should say he might," exclaimed Trent, grinning. "Seeing Beresford before breakfast! It doesn't bear thinking on."

"Lady J. thinks that by the time she and her daughter have spent a week at Vere Hall, Beresford'll have fallen in love with someone else and all will be well."

"That's probable enough. But—hell and the devil—how am I going to explain my being here, too?"

Button languorously explained that it was this question that had driven them to extreme measures. "Greater love hath no man, etcetera, my dear fellow. We understood that we had to warn you forthwith. It would have been disastrous, don't you know, to emerge from the stables, pitchfork in hand, and run smack into the Jerryhams."

"Well, I wouldn't have done. I've been promoted." As Trent explained his new occupation, his friends looked relieved.

"It's an improvement. But got to tell you, Trent, it don't seem like a thing a gentleman should be doing," Montesque opined. "Collecting rents and chucking tenants around—not ton, dear old boy. The incomparable Miss Jerryham ain't going to understand."

Trent became thoughtful. "For once, Monty, you make sense. I shall have to tell her about Longmarsh's will. Palchard said I might make a clean breast of things in an emergency. If this isn't an emergency, I don't know what is."

"Has it been awful?" Button wondered sympathetically.

About to answer that his exile had been unmitigated hell, Trent was reminded of the pleasant hour he'd just spent with the Hannays. He glanced down at Margaret's book, which he was still holding, and instead of Lavinia's golden beauty he thought of a bright, laughing, piquant face and the curve of rosy lips.

Button misinterpreted his friend's silence. "It'll be worth it, Trent. Once Miss Jerryham realizes that you have suffered for her sake— believe me, old fellow—she'll listen to your suit."

Trent registered the truth of this. He could not understand why he didn't feel more elated. Shock, he supposed.

"You'll come to an understanding," Button was droning on. "As for Lady J., once she sniffs Longmarsh's title and fortune you'll inherit eventually, she'll make sure her visit lingers not a week but a fortnight. Later she'll tell everyone in London that she came up to Vere Hall for the express purpose of having you offer for her daughter. You are sure to carry the field, don't you think so, Monty?"

Montesque sighed. "Wheel of Fortune's on the upswing for you, Trent," he observed gloomily. "It ain't for me. Got that maggoty hunt to look forward to, for one thing. Sure to sprain something or fall off my horse. And I'll probably have spasms in the bargain, too, I shouldn't wonder."

"Cook is having spasms," Nancy announced. "She swears she's going to hand in her notice, Miss Margaret."

The chambermaid's pert visage was saucier than ever, and there was a definitely martial glint in her dark eyes. Margaret, who had been on her way to return her ladyship's cape after an outing, stopped short.

"What has happened, Nancy?"

"It's that Barnaby, miss. You'd think he was a lord, the way he pushes us around. 'Out of meh way, mey good woman,' he says to Cook in her own kitchen. I'd Barnaby *him*!"

As the day of the ball approached, Barnaby and his underlings had often been at Vere Hall. Though their presence was apparently necessary—Barnaby was affecting changes that promised to quite transform the gloomy old mausoleum—Margaret tried to avoid the caterer-decorator as much as possible. Barnaby, powdered, painted, rouged, and primped into fine London clothes, made her skin crawl.

Besides, he was a bully. Yesterday, she had seen him box Noah's ears. When she had demanded to know what Noah had done, Barnaby had shrugged and thrust forth an elegant leg. "What will yew? The brat splashed water on meh pumps."

"He don't dare cross Mr. Reddington, nor yet Mrs. Pollyshot, and he's all bows and slither wi' the mistress," Nancy said shrewdly. "He acts like butter won't melt in his mouth when he's with her. So acourse she thinks he's a prime 'un. But wi' me—"

"Has he done anything to you that is improper?" Margaret demanded as Nancy stopped short.

The chambermaid's cheeks went redder. "Not he, or he'd get a proper answer from me," she said stoutly. "I'd kick him in the bollocks, I would. It's just the way he *looks* at me. And at Elsie, too, if you know what I mean."

Margaret's nod was grim. She, too, had been on the receiving end of those insolent looks. She asked where the caterer was, and Nancy tossed her head and said she didn't know. "But he's somewheres about making life miserable for someone, that's for sure."

"I'll talk to Reddington about him," Margaret decided.

She spoke stoutly, but she was not so sure that Reddington would listen. As Nancy had pointed out, Barnaby had been shrewd enough to toadeat the butler.

Even so, the female servants had to be protected. Bidding Nancy to calm Cook as best as she could, Margaret descended the great oaken staircase in search of Reddington. As she was passing the dining room, she thought she heard an odd sound. She paused to listen and the stifled cry came again.

The massive mahogany door to the dining room was half closed. Margaret gave it a push and it squeaked open to reveal a flagstoned floor, and walls hung with the trophies of past hunts. Under the truncated head of a boar stood Barnaby.

He had the protesting Elsie in his arms and was trying to kiss her.

"Stop it at once!" Margaret shouted.

Startled, Barnaby loosed Elsie, who darted past Margaret and out the door.

"How dare you assault the housemaid?" Margaret cried.

"Nothing to worry yourself abaht. Ah have assaulted nobody, Ah can assure yew." Expecting him to try to excuse himself, Margaret was astounded when Barnaby folded his arms across his chest and smirked. "Yew know how these servant gels are, Miss Hannay. They flirt and promise with their eyes, and when yew take them up on it, they fight shy."

In spite of his affectations, Barnaby was a tall, solidly built man with shoulders that owed less to padding than to his own powerful frame. His powdered and rouged face boasted a hawk-bridged nose that might have had pretensions to aristocracy, but his loose-lipped mouth was coarse and common.

Margaret felt her gorge rise as he continued in a sickeningly familiar tone, "Servants are so stewpid, don't yew think? But I dehsay yew understand."

"I wouldn't count on it."

She saw his smile slip a little at her icy tone.

"Your duties are those of a caterer and decorator," she continued. "Please remember that your authority does not extend to the servants at Vere Hall. I am sure you understand me."

His smile was entirely gone now, and his eyes had turned ugly. "Ah don't think it's up to yew to talk abaht authority, Miss Hannay. Her leddyship knows that Ah am well connected. She sets store by that. And unless Ah miss meh guess, yew hev little credit with her."

He brushed past her and out the room, leaving her with a high color and a furiously thumping heart. It took several minutes to compose herself, after which Margaret went looking for Elsie. She found the girl in the servants' hall sobbing out her story to the other servants, who had obviously been taking their tea. So engrossed was everyone that Margaret's arrival went unnoticed.

"I didn't do nofing to encourage him," Elsie was wailing. "*I didn't.* I'm a good girl, reely I am."

Reddington scolded sternly from his place of eminence at the head of the long table. "But you must have said something. You must have led the man on."

Mrs. Pollyshot frowned but did not dare to remonstrate. "We know you're a good girl," she soothed. "You didn't mean whatever it was that set him off."

She paused when she saw Margaret. Everyone rose to their feet, and Reddington bent his head in a glacial bow. "What can we do for you, Miss Hannay?"

Ignoring his repressive tone, Margaret looked the butler in the eye. "I was a witness to Barnaby's attack on Elsie. She did nothing to encourage the man—he forced his attentions on her." She described the scene, then added, "I am persuaded that he is usurping your authority."

Reddington frowned. "How do you mean?"

"The servants here are under your charge and care. Yet he beat Noah and assaulted Elsie. He is ordering the staff about as though he, not *you*, is in charge."

Reddington's scowl deepened. His wattles had begun to pinken. "But surely, since he was hired by her ladyship—"

"Lady Vere has left her staff in your hands. It has been so for many years. To whom else can the staff turn if not to you?" Margaret paused for effect. "Elsie is a blameless victim. Nancy will tell you how this Barnaby dares to ogle her. Cook will tell of his high-handed ways in her kitchen. And as for slapping Noah, that was certainly not the action of a gentleman. Only common counter-jumpers mistreat those who serve them."

When she spoke like that, Link thought admiringly, Miss Margaret looked and sounded like a great lady. Even Reddington was impressed.

"Thank you, Miss Hannay, for bringing this matter to my attention," he declaimed. "Barnaby will be dealt with."

Margaret left the kitchen confident that the problem would be addressed. But Barnaby was cunning. Before Reddington could corner him, he went to Lady Vere and bleated that Miss Hannay had made it impossible for him to fulfill his obligations at Vere Hall.

"Ah am forced to leave your leddyship's employ," he fawned, "for Ah cannot serve yew as Ah wish, meh leddy. Thet has been made impossible. Miss Hannay has turned the servants against meh."

Lady Vere, anxious for the success of her ball and always ready to believe the worst of Margaret, summoned her companion and demanded that she apologize to Barnaby instantly.

"That I will not do," Margaret cried.

Lady Vere's eyes narrowed. "You forget yourself."

Margaret's color was high, and her eyes flashed as she replied, "No, ma'am, I do not. There is no word of truth in what Barnaby has said. He has overreached himself and seeks to cover his tracks. I pray you ask Reddington for the true version of what happened."

Lady Vere flew into a passion that was checked only by the knowledge that the Jerryhams were due to arrive in a few days' time. She could not have her staff in turmoil.

With a very bad grace she rang for Reddington, who enumerated the indignities the caterer had heaped on the staff.

"That will do. Send Barnaby to me at once," Lady Vere told the butler. She was angry at the caterer for causing this mare's nest, but she also could not afford to lose his services at this late date. Furiously, she told herself that it was all Margaret's fault.

Conjecture ran high that Barnaby would be dismissed, but the caterer remained. However, Lady Vere rang such a peal over his head that he slunk out of her presence an altered man. "And," Nancy reported gleefully to Margaret later, "Mr. Reddington's been *that* cutting to him. Cowed, he is."

Margaret wasn't so sure. She was certain that Barnaby would not forget her part in his fall from grace. She was grateful when, on his future appearances at Vere Hall, he seemed to be going out of his way to avoid her.

Beyond this, she did not think of him. Lady

Vere kept her so busy that she had little time to think of anything. But one late afternoon, when she was carrying a message to the head gardener for her ladyship, a spring-scented breeze reminded her of the night that Trent had kissed her.

Instantly, memory came flooding back. Margaret stopped short. *And,* her uncompromisingly honest mind added, *that night I kissed him back.*

Trent's lips suddenly seemed as real now as they had been that night. She could almost feel his arms around her. What is the matter with me? Margaret wondered.

Instead of seeking out Flood, she made a detour into Lady Vere's topiary garden. Walking among the carefully sculpted trees usually soothed her, but today as she walked down the sandy path to the carp pond at the center of the deserted garden, her mind remained in turmoil.

She tried to reorganize her thoughts. Trent's company was enjoyable, and she was in sympathy with a gentleman down on his luck.

But, widgeon, the odious voice of her common sense sneered, if that were all, why did you want him to go on kissing you?

At that moment she felt arms slide around her waist. Margaret had been thinking so much about Trent that it did not seem strange that he had materialized suddenly and was holding her. For a moment she let herself relax into his embrace.

"Ah thought so, Ah knew yew were the type who wanted a cuddle," Barnaby's triumphant voice hissed.

Instinctively, Margaret jerked both elbows back, catching the caterer in his solar plexus. Barnaby groaned and let her go, and she turned on him like a fury.

"What do you think you are doing? You must be mad! I will have you dismissed on the instant!"

His lips pulled back from teeth that showed yellow against his white-painted face. "Not so fast, meh proud miss. Ah want something from yew first."

Before she could move, he had caught her by the arm and dragged her back into his embrace. A steely hand clamped itself across her mouth. "Now Ah've got yew where Ah want yew," Barnaby mocked.

Margaret kicked him, hard. Her heel connected with his shin and he squawked and loosened his hold on her. She broke free and began to run, but before she'd gone three steps he caught her. They struggled in the shade of a tall topiary elephant.

"No, yew don't," he snarled.

She was in trouble and knew it. She tried to knee him in the groin—a trick Russkin had taught her to use in extreme emergencies—but she had never practiced it on anyone before, and her knee didn't connect. Worse, he caught her leg and unbalanced her so that she fell backward. He fell on top of her, knocking the breath out of her and stifling her cry for help.

"Yew spoiled my game with her leddyship, didn't yew?" he panted. "Well, now it's meh turn to ruin *yew*."

She tried to twist her head away, but it did no

good. His loose lips covered hers in a suffocating kiss. Desperation gave Margaret strength. She broke from his clasp, rolled away, and jumped to her feet. He caught her ankle, but she grabbed hold of the topiary elephant's trunk and hung on for dear life. At the same time, she let out an ear-splitting scream.

"Help! The topiary!"

Cursing, Barnaby jerked at her ankle. The elephant's tree-branch trunk broke, and she fell to the ground. Barnaby loomed over her. "Damn you, let me go," she gasped.

"Ah'll let yew go when Ah've got what Ah want from yew."

Greedy hands clasped her breasts. A vicious mouth assaulted hers. Margaret could not even breathe.

There was the sound of hurried footsteps. The next moment, Barnaby was plucked away from her. Dazed, Margaret watched as Trent flung the caterer to the ground.

"If you've done assaulting women," he snarled, "maybe you'll try your hand with me."

Barnaby leaped to his feet and rushed at Trent. Fist cracked on bone. Barnaby uttered a yell of pain and clutched his face. "Meh nose. Meh nose. Yew've broke meh nose," he howled.

Ignoring him, Trent turned to Margaret. "Are you all right?"

She had managed to get to her knees, but she was shaking too hard to stand. "He— Look out!"

Barnaby's foot caught Trent in the small of the back and sent him tumbling. "You filthy brute!" Margaret shouted. Jumping to her feet, she snatched up the elephant's severed trunk and began to beat the caterer with it. "Filthy pig! Dunghill cock! You make me want to flash my hash, you damned nail!"

Trent sat up on the grass and stared. "My God," he gasped, "where did you learn that kind of language?"

Spitting and swearing, Barnaby launched himself at Trent, but a blow to the head sent the caterer reeling. A wicked uppercut knocked him off his feet.

"Famous!" Margaret applauded. "Oh, well done!"

Trent seized his prostrate adversary by the scruff of the neck and the seat of his breeches, hustled him to the carp pond, and tossed him in. Barnaby gave a howl that dissolved into gurgles as he sank into the muddy water.

"If you so much as look at Miss Hannay again," Trent vowed as Barnaby emerged, gasping and choking, "I'll flay the hide off your greasy bones."

He broke off as Link, Nancy, Elsie, and Noah came rushing into the topiary garden. The women were each armed with a broom and a mop, Link was carrying a stout stick, and Noah was holding the large pan he'd been cleaning when summoned to arms.

"So you got here in time, Mr. Trent," Link exclaimed in relief. To Margaret he explained, "I saw this here gowp skulking into the too-pi-airy gardens, and I was sure I'd seen you go that way yourself, so when I saw Mr. Trent, I told him about it."

"Ah will have the law on yew," Barnaby spluttered. He had emerged from the carp pond and was hauling himself back onto dry land. Blood gushed from his nose, and a water lily was dangling from his ear. His expensive London clothes were covered with mud. "Ah will have yew behind bars," he threatened.

"Garn," Noah shouted. "Tyburn-bait!"

"Nasty, wicked creetur," Elsie added. Then, surprised at her own courage, she ducked behind Nancy.

"Think anyone'll listen to yer, yer loose fish?" Nancy jeered.

"Her leddyship will. She won't believe a word yew say." Barnaby tested his nose and added maliciously, "And if I say the word, Miss Hannay will be disgraced."

Trent realized that Barnaby had the right of it. Margaret's name must not be bandied about.

He stalked over to the caterer, grasped him by his soggy lapels, and shook him savagely. By contrast, his voice was almost gentle as he said, "Mention one word of what has happened today and, by God, I'll break your neck. Keep your mouth shut and you *might* escape with a whole skin. Believe me, I never make idle threats."

Barnaby's bluster collapsed. Mumbling compliance, he hung loosely in Trent's grip until he was released. Then he slunk off. The squishing sound his pumps made seemed to give Noah great pleasure, and he ran after Barnaby howling with glee and pounding his pan with his fist. Nancy and Elsie followed, but Trent called Link back.

Holding out his hand, he said, "Thank you for warning me that Miss Hannay was in trouble."

Link reddened, shook hands awkwardly, and muttered that he'd been doing his duty.

"I told you I'd let you know if there was trouble, sir." He turned to Margaret. "If you're sure you're all right, miss?"

Margaret's lips were trembling a little as she smiled. "Yes, thanks to you," she said. Link went even redder and grinned all over his face as he left the garden. Margaret now turned to Trent. *"Deus ex machina,"* she murmured.

"What? Oh, I see. The god from the machine. Though there wasn't anything godlike about it. I was riding up to the house and saw Link racing past. He yelled something about your needing help in the topiary garden, so—"

She interrupted, "So Sir Trent came to the rescue. And this time there *was* a dragon."

Gently tilting her chin, he looked down into her face. "You're confoundedly pale. We'd best sit down."

He slid a supporting arm around her, then led her to a marble seat set under the outstretched wings of a topiary eagle. "Not feeling faint, are you?" he asked anxiously.

"It was so sudden. I did not expect the assault. I hadn't thought he would dare. And when he put his arms around me—" She broke off, but her mind continued the words. When *Barnaby put his arms around me, I thought it was you.*

Noting the tremble in her voice, Trent gritted, "I should have drowned him."

"I'm glad you didn't. No matter how odious he is, Lady Vere would not wish to lose his services so close to her guests' arrival, and she would have blamed me." She gave a quavery chuckle and added, "You put the fear of God into him, however. He'll not dare to try his tricks again."

"He'd better not. If he so much as looks at you, I'll . . . God, it makes me feel sick to think what might have happened if I hadn't been nearby."

He tightened his arm around her shoulders, and Margaret was so tempted to lean into its comforting strength that she was frightened.

She hastily drew away from temptation and said cheerfully, "Let us not talk about Barnaby anymore. I collect that you said you were riding up to Vere Hall when you saw Link. Are you here on business for Mr. Block?"

Trent shook his head. "I came to see you."

She tried to quell the leap of her pulse. And failed. Her heart had begun to beat much more swiftly than it had done under Barnaby's attack.

"To see . . . me?"

He'd meant to continue, but when he looked down into her upturned face, everything went out of his mind.

When he'd seen Margaret on the ground with Barnaby on top of her, Trent had felt a rage such as he had never before experienced. The memory of it made him demand, "Are you sure you're all right?"

"If you ask me once more, I will faint dead at your feet," she vowed, "and then you will be forced to burn feathers under my nose and run for restoratives. It will serve you right."

He grinned with relief. "You look more the thing now. And you sound like yourself, too.

When I think of you batting away at Barnaby with that tree branch—"

With a gasp of dismay, Margaret jumped to her feet and picked up the branch. "Oh, Lord. What will Flood say? He is so fond of his trees. No," she added as Trent gave a shout of laughter, "it's terribly serious."

"Flood should be honored to think that his tree helped you to defend yourself," Trent said. "What's a tree compared to a beautiful lady?"

"What did you say?" Margaret whispered.

About to give her a light reply, Trent stopped short at the look in her eyes. He tried to speak, but there seemed to be something caught in his throat. She *was* beautiful. Beautiful and brave and dear.

Suddenly, he recalled his reason for visiting Vere Hall. Trent gave his forgetful mind a slap and lurched into an explanation.

"Miss Hannay, I came here to tell you—it's about those visitors who are coming to Vere Hall. One of them is Miss Jerryham." She looked at him blankly and he blurted, "You know, Miss Jerre."

She had been attempting to push the elephant's trunk back into place. Now she went quite still. Not noticing this, he continued, "Miss Jerryham will be visiting with her mother."

"Oh. I see."

Margaret spoke so calmly, so indifferently even, that the wind was taken out of Trent's sails. "I thought I'd tell you," he said awkwardly. "Thought you'd want to know, I mean."

She asked in that same distant voice, "Did you only recently learn that she was coming here?"

"Exactly. Button and Monty came out to warn, er, tell me. Miss Jerryham doesn't know I'm here, you see."

"You mean that she does not realize that you were a groom and have now been promoted to assistant land steward." Margaret turned to face him. "You must be very happy that she is coming."

She looked pale again, and Trent cursed himself for a fool. The poor girl was still in shock from Barnaby's attack.

Going up to her, he caught her hands. They felt very cold. "I'm an idiot," he said contritely. "You've had a great scare and here I'm blabbering on about the Jerryhams' visit. Let me take you to the hall. You should lie down."

She hardly heard him. The fact that Miss Jerryham was Trent's Miss Jerre solely occupied Margaret's mind. It was only with great effort that she managed to say, "I don't need to lie down. I am going to say good night to her ladyship and then go home to Mama."

"I'll walk with you," he offered.

"Please don't. It would cause talk if you hung about waiting for me, and Lady Vere will twit me for it. Really, I am all right. And thank you for telling me about Miss Jerre—Miss Jerryham. I will make every effort to see to her comfort."

Trent was indignant. "I didn't tell you so that you could take care of her!" he exclaimed. "There're servants enough for that."

The eyes that met his were cold. "I, too, am a servant at Vere Hall."

For some reason Trent felt himself on the defensive. "Dash it, it's not what I meant, and you know it. I told you about Miss Jerryham because I didn't want her coming to be a surprise."

"How very kind of you."

Hazel eyes locked with green. "Well," Trent burst out, "I didn't expect this from you."

Margaret didn't recognize her own voice. It sounded silky and soft but as cold as ice. "No?"

"No, confound it! When Monty told me she was coming, my first thought was of you. No, I'm not bamming you," he added when he saw her eyes narrow. "Here you were under that horrible woman's thumb and there wasn't anyone to help you. I thought that Miss Jerryham could take your part." She said nothing. "I thought," he ended lamely, "that you would be glad she was coming."

Margaret closed her eyes for a moment. The struggle she waged was a silent one. When she opened her eyes again, they were clear, and she even managed a smile.

"I *am* glad for you," she said. "Pray forgive me. I am still a little overwrought, I think." She held out her hand. "Friends?"

He clasped it eagerly and then, moved by something he did not understand, raised it to his lips. Her skin was silk-soft and fragrant. It reminded him of the taste of her lips.

Suddenly, the memory of that night came roaring back and jostled aside all other considerations. Trent knew he didn't want to shake hands with Margaret. He wanted to pull her into his arms and kiss her.

Thoroughly shaken, he let go of her hand. *Miss Jerryham was his true love!*

Trent put his hands behind his back and drew himself erect. He sent a smile in Margaret's general direction.

"Yes," he agreed heartily. "Exactly. Friends."

Chapter Seven

Reddington's stern eyes appraised the servants. Always a martinet, he had never before been so severe. This was, after all, to be his last inspection before the Jerryhams' arrival.

Lady Vere's servants were washed, brushed, and combed, and their liveries, dresses, caps, gloves, and aprons were spotless. Even Noah, standing at the very end of the long line, looked almost clean.

It was a fine day in May. The domestic staff had assembled out of doors and were grouped at the foot of the steps that led to the house. Margaret watched the domestic lineup from the morning-room window, where she had been stationed by Lady Vere.

The servants were the only people in sight. Though every few minutes Lady Vere demanded to know whether her guests were coming, Margaret kept answering that she could not see anyone.

"They are late. They should have been here an hour since," Lady Vere fretted. "Look again."

Margaret searched the wide road that led to Vere Hall and could now discern a puff of dust in the distance. "I believe that they are coming," she exclaimed.

"Well, don't just stand there, then! Fetch me my mirror."

Margaret hastened to bring a silver-backed mirror so that Lady Vere could admire herself. Tricked out in a jaconet muslin dress of silver-gray, with pearls in her ears and her fair hair arranged in the Roman style, Lady Vere looked quite the thing.

By contrast, Margaret looked like a dowd. On her ladyship's orders she had put on a high-necked dress of a greenish color that could only be described as dead leaf green. Her hair had been skinned back and bundled into a tight knot at the back of her head.

"Go back to the window and tell me what is happening," Lady Vere commanded.

From her vantage point, Margaret watched the traveling carriage carrying Lady Jerryham and her daughter wheel into the courtyard. The carriage was followed by a chaise, which contained the ladies' abigails and the baggage. Bringing up the rear of the procession was Lady Jerryham's younger brother, the Honorable Vincent Federby.

Since Sir Bartholomew had refused point-blank to go jauntering off to God-knows-where to taste some bilious mineral water, Federby had consented to act as escort. Driving his curricle, which was drawn by two matched bays, he was in the crack of fashion with his bright blue coat with layers of shoulder padding, tight buff breeches, and a magnificent cravat done in the waterfall style, which completely eclipsed his chin.

"Can you see Miss Jerryham?" Lady Vere gave Margaret a look of spiteful satisfaction as she added, "She is a famous beauty and dresses exquisitely. You can learn a lesson in fashion from her."

Margaret made an equable answer. She was glad that Miss Jerryham's name did not cause her even the smallest twinge of discomfort. This proved that her reaction to Trent's announcement had been the result of surprise and the shock of the now completely chastened Barnaby's attack.

"The carriages are now at the door, ma'am," she told Lady Vere.

The traveling carriage had stopped, the chaise had lumbered to a standstill, and the bays drawing Federby's curricle had halted. As Link ran forward to lower the carriage steps, Lady Vere rose majestically and swept out of the morning room and down the grand stairs to the ground-floor anteroom. Margaret followed at a respectful distance.

Link pulled open the outer door with a flourish, and Lady Vere stepped onto the topmost outer step to greet her guests.

"My dear Charlotte!"

"Dear, dear Alice! It has been so long!"

The ladies embraced, aiming kisses in the air above each other's ears.

Standing a few steps behind her employer, Margaret watched silently. Her eyes were not on the richly dressed Lady Jerryham or her dandified brother, but on the exquisite young lady who was coming up the stairs. Trent had described Miss Jerryham as beautiful, but, Margaret thought, he hadn't done her justice.

Lavinia Jerryham was the loveliest woman Margaret had ever seen. Her oval face, perfect in every feature, was dominated by large blue eyes, and her rosebud lips parted to disclose pearllike teeth.

Her beauty was enhanced by a sky-blue velvet pelisse trimmed with ermine and a matching white ermine muff. A single ostrich plume curled saucily about the brim of a sky-blue hat that framed her golden curls. Suddenly made conscious of her own appearance, Margaret smoothed a hand over her dress.

"Let me present my daughter, Charlotte," Lady Jerryham was saying. Triumphantly she added, "I collect that you have not seen her for many years. Has Lavinia not changed?"

"And *how* have you changed, dear Lavinia. Such beauty. Such address," gushed Lady Vere. "Alice, you must be proud to be the mother of such a lovely creature. Come and kiss me, my dear child."

A flicker of movement near the topiary garden caught Margaret's attention. She glanced sideways and saw Trent standing in the shadow of the trees. He wore a new coat of brown superfine and fawn-colored breeches, and his dark head was unpowdered and as glossy as a raven's wing.

Naturally he hadn't been able to wait for a glimpse of his ladylove. Margaret's heart, which had been schooled to submission, gave a rebellious start. Before she could get it under control, Trent turned his head and looked directly at her.

He had left Beau tethered nearby and walked to the topiary garden. He had meant to feast his eyes on Lavinia, to try to catch her eye so that he could arrange a meeting with her. And when he had first seen her step out of the carriage, her beauty had dazzled him, and he had greedily savored the details of her perfection.

Trent had admired Lavinia's exquisite golden hair, the harmony of her costly costume, her graceful little gestures. And then, inexplicably, instinctively, he had looked for Margaret.

He saw her standing behind Lady Vere in the open doorway, and even he had to admit that she looked like a drudge. Then she turned toward him and their eyes came together with the click of magnets, and the transformation occurred.

Trent felt as though the sky had opened and a thunderbolt had fallen on him. Vivid, vital, *alive*, Margaret's beauty shone like the morning star. My God, Trent thought, stunned. There's no one who can touch her—not even Lavinia.

He shook his head as though to clear it, but he remained dazzled. Feature by feature, there was no comparison between the women. But though Lavinia Jerryham was wondrously fair, marvelously graceful, and exquisitely dressed, Trent couldn't keep his eyes away from Margaret. Under his gaze, he saw her cheeks flush, her lips part. Unconsciously, he took a step toward her.

At that moment, Lavinia chanced to glance over her shoulder. Her eyes, glazed with boredom, suddenly grew gimlet-keen. What on earth was Mr. Kenneth Trenton doing *here*?

Her first thought was that her admirer had followed her from London, but that flattering notion ebbed swiftly. Not only had Mr. Trenton been absent from her circle for some time, but she also realized that something had changed. He was not driving his curricle, for one thing. He wore clothes that were too subdued to be fashionable. And he was behaving in a most peculiar way.

Lavinia frowned. Instead of giving her his entire attention, Kenneth Trenton was staring at the red-haired woman who stood behind Lady Vere, the one who was dressed like a frump and who was obviously some kind of servant.

She touched Lady Vere's hand and inquired sweetly, "Pray, dear Lady Vere, make me known to that pleasant young person yonder."

Her ladyship made a withering answer. "Margaret Hannay acts as my companion."

Lavinia's sharp ears picked up Lady Vere's contemptuous tone. She then assessed the grace with which Margaret Hannay curtsied. Her flowerlike mouth pursed thoughtfully, and she glanced once more at the spot where Kenneth Trenton had stood. He wasn't there any longer.

How odd, Lavinia thought.

Margaret, too, was aware that Trent had gone. She was grateful, for his presence had confused her. When he had looked at her a moment ago, she had felt as breathless as if she had run for miles. But Trent had come to see Miss Jerryham. Then why—

"Miss Hannay?"

She looked up quickly and met lovely sky-blue eyes. "Ma'am?" she stammered.

Lavinia's laugh was like the tinkle of silvery

bells. "Oh, please, not 'ma'am.' We are nearly of an age. We will be friends."

Charmed, Margaret said frankly, "I would like that above all things."

Behind her smile, Lavinia was chagrined to note that when she smiled, this companion creature was quite pretty. But surely Mr. Trenton could not be so lost to propriety as to dangle after a mere lady's companion!

Contemptuously, Lavinia dismissed that notion. It was far more likely that the handsome young man had heard she was coming to Vere Hall and followed her. Lavinia dimpled, well pleased. Though neither she nor her parents had ever considered Kenneth Trenton to be a serious suitor, he would help to assuage the boredom at Vere Hall.

I must speak to him, Lavinia decided.

This was not difficult to arrange. Trent was finding it difficult to drag himself away from Vere Hall. He was still standing near Beau and telling himself that he must leave when Lavinia's abigail ran out and slipped a note into his hand.

"Meet me in the topiary garden," the note said, "in half an hour. I will try to get away."

Trent kissed the note in true loverlike fashion. Now, he was sure, the world would return to sanity. It was, after all, Miss Jerryham who held his worshipful soul while Miss Hannay was . . . well, she was just Margaret.

For the life of him he could not understand why she, in that unsightly dress and with her hair skinned back, could have caught at his heart a few moments ago. He was still vibrating from the shock. It was confoundedly puzzling and confusing. But now that he was to see his Lavinia, all would be well.

Trent went into the topiary garden to wait. It was a mistake. The minute he'd set eyes on the trunkless elephant he recalled how Margaret had seized that branch and beaten Barnaby with it while calling him unrepeatable names.

Suddenly, Margaret seemed everywhere. He could see her whooping like a savage in the meadow, or wrestling with the rusty old pump outside her cottage, or showing him how to mend a pitchfork.

Even memories of Margaret were unorthodox. "Plague take the girl." Trent sighed.

"Mr. Trenton?"

He turned with relief toward a vision of loveliness. Lavinia had removed her pelisse and wore a day dress of blue sprigged muslin. The stand-up collar of her short spencer framed her face to perfection. Her fair hair was gloriously bare, and sunlight glinted on a profusion of curls.

She was so beautiful. Trent recalled a time when, at her country home, he had fallen on his knees at her feet. She had smiled adorably at him then and murmured that he must not put her to the blush.

She was smiling now. "Why are you staring at me, Mr. Trenton?" she cooed. "I vow that you will put me to the blush."

Lavinia's long lashes fluttered like butterflies' wings. Trent could swear that he'd never seen such lovely blue orbs, yet the eyes that persistently came to mind were hazel.

Trent gave himself a savage mental shake.

"I'm staring at you because you're so lovely, Miss Jerryham," he said.

She snapped open her fan of alençon lace and held it up to half conceal her face. It was a gesture that Lavinia had perfected after many hours of practice before her mirror.

"I am persuaded you are joking me," she murmured. "Why have you not come near me for the past two months?"

Over the fan's rim, her eyes promised him the world. Trent said fervently, "One month and twenty-seven days. I've counted them, Miss Jerryham. They've been an eternity, I promise you."

Lavinia lowered her fan and gave him a smile that would have melted a glacier. "Deceiver." She pouted. "I collect that you forgot about me."

"Forgot! Now that," Trent exclaimed earnestly, "is doing it too brown. It was for you that I came to Longmarsh."

Blue eyes widened with keen interest. "You are visiting Longmarsh? We heard that the old earl had died. Can it be that you are acquainted with his heir?"

Trent drew a deep breath and attempted to collect his thoughts. Since Button and Montesque had materialized out of the twilight to pass on their news, he had been considering the best way in which to reveal the truth. Mentally, he had written several scenarios and had finally settled on one. But this morning's events had knocked the words out of his brain.

Lavinia scarcely noticed his silence. "Since the old earl died, we have been agog with curiosity. Mama said this morning, as we passed Longmarsh, that the earldom is to go to a great-nephew. How fortunate he will be."

Thankful that she had given him a way of broaching the subject, Trent spoke offhandedly. "Oh, I suppose Longmarsh's not a bad place."

Lavinia clapped her hands. "Then you *are* a guest of the new earl! Cruel man, to leave London without telling us. And why did you not come and greet us when we arrived here? How glad Mama will be if you could introduce us to the new Lord Longmarsh."

This was getting complicated. "I can't," Trent said. "At least, not yet."

"I do not understand," Lavinia protested.

"It's a long story. Perhaps if we sit down?" He led her toward the marble seat and was captured by tendrils of memory. Margaret looking up into his eyes, Margaret leaning momentarily into his arm. . . . "Stop that," Trent muttered.

"I beg your pardon?"

"I wasn't talking to you, I was—" Trent broke off to clear his throat. "You see, it all started when the late earl wrote a will. In it he said that in order to inherit the bulk of Longmarsh's fortune, his heir had to—to fulfill certain conditions. Rather like the labors of Hercules." Seeing an uncomprehending look cross Lavinia's flawless face, he paused to explain, "Hercules was a Greek chap who had several tasks set for him by a king. One was to go and steal a dog from the underworld. Pernicious kind of hound, with lots of teeth on account of the fact that he had three heads."

"I vow that I do not understand one word you are saying."

Trent had broken into a light sweat. "Another

121

of Hercules' labors was to capture the old man of the sea." Lavinia's foot began to tap the ground. "A third," he went on desperately, "was to clean out some stables. That's where Longmarsh's will comes in."

Lavinia rose to her feet. "You are hoaxing me," she said icily. "I will return to the house."

He caught her hand, and she looked down at him in surprise. Kenneth Trenton had definitely changed. The old Mr. Trenton, the admirer she had meant to tease and trifle with, would never have dared to take her hand so boldly. Lavinia decided that this new focefulness definitely made him more interesting.

Trent was saying, "Longmarsh's will stipulated that in order to inherit the money needed to run the estate, his heir should work at Longmarsh for a year. His first task was to clean out the stables."

Lavinia's fine eyebrows nearly disappeared into her fringe of curls. "You cannot mean to tell me Longmarsh wished his heir to work as a *groom*?"

Vastly relieved, Trent nodded. "Exactly so. Deucedly clever of you, Miss Jerryham. But he—the heir—didn't stay a groom very long. I—he, I mean—was promoted to an assistant land steward shortly afterward."

Lavinia's bewildered look disappeared, and her eyes became shrewd and bright.

"You said 'I' just now. You cannot mean . . . Are *you* Longmarsh's heir?" He nodded diffidently, and she sank back onto the stone seat. With her eyes fixed on his face, she gasped, "*You* are the new Earl of Longmarsh! Why did you not tell me?" Her smile had come back, more bewitching than before, and she archly tapped his arm with her fan. "You ran away from London without a word. I was persuaded that you had taken me in dislike. Now I learn that you are the new earl."

"Upon my word," he began, but she interrupted.

Eyelashes fluttering, she charged, "But of course in your dignity as the new Lord Longmarsh you forsook your friends."

He thought of himself up to his boot tops in dirty straw. He thought of Jennings's vitriolic tongue.

"Confess, you forgot me."

Lavinia's soft voice caressed the words, and her eyes issued an invitation he couldn't resist. Trent slid an arm around her slender waist and tried to kiss her. She evaded his arms but gave him her hand instead.

"I've thought of you constantly."

Even the way he kissed her hand had changed! Lavinia's eyelashes fluttered with more excitement than art as she murmured, "Perhaps you found another's company more congenial to mine. Lady Vere's companion is an odd creature, to be sure, but she might appeal to some."

Trent felt as if she had thrown cold water into his face.

"Now, what was her name?" Lavinia was wondering. "Oh, yes. Hannay. Lady Vere said that she was a soldier's daughter."

"Captain Hannay was in the dragoon guards," Trent said.

She did not miss the stiffness in his voice and changed her tactics. "You see? I knew you had forgotten me. Odious creature," she added caressingly, "after all your promises of devotion. But men are ever thus."

"It's important that you understand," he insisted. "Miss Hannay and her mother are my friends. I can't explain how much that has meant. By the terms of my great-uncle's will, I was a groom when I met the Hannays. I was below their touch, of course, but they made me welcome in their home."

He saw that Lavinia was staring at him fixedly. "Margaret—Miss Hannay, I mean—is a fine person, but Lady Vere treats her abominably. She went so far as to box Mar—Miss Hannay's ears, and it made me furious because I was helpless, I was hoping that you would . . . well—"

Lavinia was surprised. "You were hoping that I might befriend her?"

"Yes, that's it. I knew you would understand." Eagerly, Trent caught her hand and squeezed it.

It was worse than she had thought. When she first saw Kenneth Trenton throw sheep's eyes at the Hannay creature, Lavinia had been piqued because she saw a devoted admirer, however unsuitable, slipping away from her orbit. She had not known *then* that he was the Earl of Longmarsh. She glanced at Trent under her long eyelashes and noted all the qualities that had recommended him even when he was an ineligible suitor. His height, the breadth of his shoulders, those darkly handsome features, and those smoldering green eyes . . .

Lavinia's own eyes narrowed. As the Earl of Longmarsh, the man would be the catch of the Season. All of the matchmaking mamas in London would set their caps for him.

He must declare himself before she left Vere Hall, she decided. Surely it would not be difficult to get an offer out of him?

"I will do everything I can," Lavinia said firmly.

Trent's green eyes burned with gratitude. "You'll speak to Miss Hannay then?"

"Oh, yes," she promised. "I will certainly do that."

Vastly relieved, Trent kissed her hand again. Lavinia considered letting him kiss her lips but rejected the idea. It was broad daylight and their conversation had been much too centered around that odious Hannay creature. In order to burn her kiss into Trenton's mind, she would have to set the stage.

"Please," she murmured, "leave me now. Mama will wonder where I am, and it will not do for anyone to see the two of us leaving the garden together." Her eyelashes fluttered devastatingly. "Later we will talk again."

After Trent had gone, Lavinia sat for some moments in deep thought. Then, snapping shut her fan, she rose and walked briskly toward the house. As she did so, she chanced to look up and saw Margaret standing at a window. She was watching Trent leave, and her heart was in her eyes.

Lavinia began to smile. No, she thought, it would not be hard at all.

She was humming to herself as she approached the house. When Link opened the door, she asked where Miss Hannay might be. Then following Link's directions, Lavinia went to the morning room.

Margaret had been sent there to fetch Lady Vere's embroidery but had stayed to watch Trent emerging from the topiary garden. An ache had begun somewhere under her rib cage when she saw his blissful expression. Had he kissed Miss Jerryham by the carp pond? Had he put his arms around her as he had done to Margaret that day when Barnaby had attacked her?

"Dolt," Margaret hissed to herself. "Pea-goose. Gudgeon."

She turned from the window and banged her shin against the heavy lattice-back chair. The pain was so bad that tears came, and she closed her eyes against them. Margaret was grateful for the physical pain that took her mind away from the other, more insistent ache.

Trent had been honest about loving Lavinia Jerryham. She had known all along where his affections lay. It was no use crying over milk that was bound to be spilled, Margaret told herself.

The door to the morning room opened and Lavinia came in. "I have been looking for you." Lavinia smiled.

Margaret blinked. "Ma'am?"

Lavinia crossed the floor to Margaret. "I want you to be the first to wish me happy," she confided.

"Oh!"

The word seemed to be torn out of Margaret. Lavinia's eyes widened with blue candor. "You do wish me happy, don't you?"

Margaret nodded dumbly.

Lavinia took Margaret's cold hand and clasped it. "Mr. Trenton must have told you about our feelings for one another."

"Yes, he told me." *Mr. Trenton* . . . So even his name had been a lie. He wasn't Ken Trent at all, Margaret thought sadly.

She knew nothing about this Mr. Trenton—nothing at all except that she had felt so close to him that she could laugh and talk without pretense. She knew nothing of him except that his kisses had been burned into her heart.

Now he had offered for this beautiful, wealthy, and well-connected lady. Margaret saw that Lavinia was watching her and managed to stretch her lips into a smile. "I know how dearly he has loved you, ma'am. Your name was always on his lips."

"We will be married when he comes into his inheritance." Lavinia saw that Margaret looked bewildered and decided that it was now time to administer the *coup de grace*. "Surely he has told you that he's the new Earl of Longmarsh?"

"The Earl of Longmarsh!"

As the words exploded from Margaret's lips, Lavinia grasped her arm and half dragged her back to the window. It gave a good view of the westerly boundary of Lady Vere's property. Beyond this boundary lay Longmarsh's land.

Lavinia looked at the green acres possessively. "A lovely estate, isn't it?"

"He never told me that he was the earl." Margaret spoke as though to herself. "I thought that he was running away from London because of a duel, that he was disguising himself as a groom for fear of discovery."

A trill of laughter cut short her stammerings. "A duel! Fear of discovery! Oh, my dear, you should pen a romance, indeed you should." She paused and added seriously, "It really is too bad that Kenneth did not tell you, especially since he professes to feel such friendship toward you."

Margaret stood stock-still as Lavinia's sugared voice explained the conditions of the late earl's will. "Who is to know what bee the old man had in his bonnet? It is most irregular to have one's heir work on his own estate, but Kenneth is enduring all this for my sake." She paused. "You are very pale. Are you well, Miss Hannay?"

"I am quite well," Margaret said in a low voice. "I am surprised, that is all."

"He swore me to secrecy, for no one knows who he is. But I had to tell you," Lavinia paused complacently. "You are such great friends, after all . . ."

She let the sentence drift into a question, and the look in her blue eyes pierced Margaret's wretchedness.

"I hope," Lavinia went on, "that you will not think me bold when I say that I am grateful to you and your mother for befriending Kenneth. Your company may well have kept him from—I shall not peel eggs with you—temptations of a base nature." Lavinia lowered her voice. "Gentlemen can be so odious. They profess to love you, but out of sight, out of mind. And they *will* form attachments with unsuitable females. Naturally, it is only a diversion and means nothing, but it is highly provoking."

"You have no need for concern." Margaret's voice was now fully under control. "You can be sure that Mr. Trent . . . that Mr. Trenton is an honorable gentleman. His heart has always belonged to you."

Surprised at Margaret's composure, Lavinia saw that the woman was actually smiling. She began to wonder if she had made a mistake. Perhaps Trenton and this lady's companion *were* only friends.

Lavinia had no way of knowing what Margaret's smile cost her.

"I wish you very happy, indeed, Miss Jerryham," Margaret continued. "Now, if you will excuse me, Lady Vere is waiting for her embroidery."

Chapter Eight

"Young Trenton, the Earl of Longmarsh? Lavinia, have you had too much sun?"

Lady Jerryham's eyes resembled small black currants protruding from a bread pudding. Lavinia surveyed her mother calmly.

"I am neither sun-struck nor queer in the attic, Mama. Mr. Trenton is indeed Longmarsh's heir. It seems that he must prove himself before inheriting the late earl's money, but inherit it he will."

Lady Jerryham sank back into her chair and began to fan herself so hard that locks of artificially darkened hair blew across her face.

"It must a Banbury story!" she exclaimed. "*Why* should the old earl choose Kenneth Trenton as his heir?"

"I don't know, Mama, but that is the way it is."

Lady Jerryham stared hard at her daughter. "Has he offered for you?" she asked bluntly.

"Not yet. But," Lavinia pointed out reasonably, "why would he tell me his secret if he wasn't going to ask me to marry him? He said that he has kept it a secret from everyone. Even the Hannay creature didn't know."

"The Hannay . . . Oh, Charlotte's companion. What has she got to do with Trenton, pray?"

A small pucker drew Lavinia's brows together. "He says they're friends."

"Friends! An earl and a lady's companion? You are joking me, Lavinia." Lady Jerryham closed her fan with a decisive snap. "*Friendship* is not the word I would use in this case. Men will be men, after all. But if that young woman thinks she can entrap an earl, she is rainbow-chasing."

Lavinia smiled.

"It is true that young Trenton is well connected," Lady Jerryham continued. "His grandfather was a baron, and his mother was one of the Scottish Blairs, a very acceptable family. As the Earl of Longmarsh, he will be a most desirable catch."

Mother and daughter exchanged speaking glances. Then Lady Jerryham announced, "I must inform Charlotte at once."

Lavinia looked alarmed. "Lady Vere is a prattlebox. She'll tell everyone in the county."

"Charlotte is one of my oldest friends and I know her very well. She is a toadeater. She will keep her tongue still so that she can tell everyone, *later*, that she was the first to entertain the Earl of Longmarsh at her ball."

"I understand, Mama."

"You will wear your new gown," Lady Jerryham went on. "You will look magnificent. If Trenton doesn't offer for you that very evening, I will be very much surprised." She paused. "But I have another reason for telling Charlotte. There is a matter in which I require her assistance."

Lavinia asked what this matter might be. Lady Jerryham explained. "Oh, yes, Mama, I am persuaded that you are right." Lavinia then dimpled. "You think of everything."

Some time later, Margaret was summoned to the morning room and found Nancy pretending to dust in the hall. The chambermaid put a finger to her lips.

"They're in there, all three o' them," she whispered. "Something's going on, miss. When I took the tea in, they had their heads together, as thick as thieves, wi' the mistress looking fit to bust. 'How can such a thing be?' she says. 'I called him a gapeseed,' she says."

"So she did," Margaret mused. "And other things besides."

"Then you know what they're yammering about?" Like an inquisitive, black-eyed magpie, Nancy cocked her head to one side.

Lavinia must have announced her engagement to the new Earl of Longmarsh. Margaret suddenly felt weary. The last thing she wanted to do was to go into the morning room, but she had no choice.

She managed a smile. "You had better be careful. Reddington is on the prowl. I saw him on the stairs."

Nancy hastily whisked herself off, and Margaret knocked on the morning-room door. She was told to enter. "And shut the door behind you," Lady Vere commanded.

Her ladyship's voice was sharper than ever. She had had the shock of her life and needed to vent her spleen.

"You knew about this." When Margaret shook her head, Lady Vere spluttered, "Insolent gel.

You knew all along that Trenton was Long-marsh."

"Mr. Trenton did not confide in me, ma'am." Lady Vere snorted her disbelief. "Miss Jerryham will tell you how amazed I was when she told me the news."

Before Lavinia could speak, Lady Vere charged, "You two appeared to be bosom bows. I saw you looking at him in such a way—oh pray, don't blush, I am no fool. And still you tell me you knew nothing about his title?"

Not trusting herself to speak, Margaret shook her head.

"Talking will not mend fences," Lady Jerryham interposed. "The important thing, Charlotte, is that the earl—or Mr. Trenton as I suppose he must be called for the time being—receive an invitation immediately."

"Fetch me my pen and writing materials," Lady Vere snapped at Margaret.

As Margaret left the room, she saw Lavinia watching her with what she took for sympathy. This should have made her feel better, but it did not. Margaret's steps, as she walked down the long flagstone hallway, echoed mournfully in her ears. "I saw you look at him in such a way . . ." Lady Vere had said, and the hell of it was that her ladyship was right.

Why didn't he tell me? she wondered.

Elsie's voice intruded into her thoughts. "Are you all right, miss? You're looking ever so funny."

"Am I really? I'm in a hurry, that is all."

"She's got you on the hop again," Elsie sympathized. "You ain't the only one neither. She had Mr. Reddington in there afore now, and he come out looking as though she'd handed him a jaw-me-dead. Then Mr. Reddington shouted for Link, and off *he* had to go as though the witches were arter him. I wonder what's going on?"

Margaret merely shook her head. She found and carried the writing materials back to Lady Vere and, finding her alone in the morning room, braced herself for a storm. Her mistress, however, was too distracted to do more than instruct her to wait while the invitation was written.

"Tell Reddington to have it delivered to my lord directly." Now it was 'my lord,' Margaret observed. "There is little time, for the ball is to be held this week." Lady Vere sealed the envelope and grumbled, "It is an awkward business. The first time the earl is to enter Vere Hall, and none of his friends will be invited. But they are no doubt all in London and cannot come at such short notice."

Margaret remembered Messrs. Montesque and Butterworth. "Two of his friends are staying at Norsby with Lord and Lady Korrowin," she offered.

Lady Vere pounced on this news, but could not resist adding, "Good God, I will be obliged to invite Korrowin and his wife and their antidote of a daughter, too." She pushed out her underlip. "So you are acquainted with the new earl's London friends, are you? What toploftly company you keep these days. I collect that soon you will grow too fine to remain in my employ."

Goaded beyond bearing, Margaret cried, "Is your ladyship dissatisfied with me? If so, I beg you to tell me frankly. I am not one to beat about the bush."

Delighted that she had upset her young companion, Lady Vere sniffed. "Highty-tighty, why fly up into the boughs? Sit down and wait while I write to the Korrowins and their guests."

After the invitations were written, Margaret went down to the servants' hall in search of Reddington and was told that he was taking tea with Mrs. Pollyshot in the housekeeper's parlor. Rather than disturb them, Margaret instructed Link to deliver the invitations immediately.

The underfootman grumbled. "That's the second time I had to drive out to Longmarsh this day. First time, it was a letter to that there Mr. Block. Now this."

"What's in the letter then, Miss Margaret?" Nancy wanted to know.

A senior footman told her to hold her tongue. Undaunted, Nancy tossed her head. "Looks like one o' them invitations to the ball as went out to the gentry some time past," she guessed.

"Garn," Noah scoffed. "The mistress ain't going to invite no groom, even if 'e's reely a gentry mort, to 'er bleeding ball."

"Mind your manners, you," Nancy snapped. "Now, Miss Margaret, isn't this here letter an invitation?"

Conscious of all eyes upon her, Margaret nodded, and Link slapped his hand down on the table. "He's got to be a lord in disguise. Why else would the mistress invite him an' all?"

Elsie clasped her hands together and said that it was like a story her mam had told her.

"Like Cinderella, Mr. Trent is, wi' a fairy godmother," she said, sighing, whereat Noah began to mince and swish about the room.

"Oo, I'm a fairy godmother," he squeaked. "I grant wishes, I does."

"What is the meaning of this foolery?"

Reddington had stalked into the servants' hall. His wattles were red and quivering, and his quelling glare reduced his underlings to an uneasy silence. Then he bowed frostily to Margaret and begged to know the reason for her appearance belowstairs.

When told, Reddington was too conscious of his position to show surprise. Instead, he glared at Link and bellowed, "Why are you lingering? Depart at once and carry out her ladyship's orders."

Peter Link flew out the doors. Noah started to scrub pots as if his life depended on it. The senior footman mumbled that he had something to attend to and nearly collided with Nancy, who was also making herself scarce. Watching the staff scurry like mice under Reddington's baleful gaze, Margaret could hardly suppress her laughter.

She managed to keep a straight face until she was out of the servants' hall. She then escaped upstairs into the picture gallery, shut the door, and let loose the first laugh she had had that day. She laughed as she recalled Reddington's expression, the way Noah had scuttled for the pots, the look on Link's face as he took flight. She howled until tears streamed from her eyes.

"Are you laughing or crying?"

Where had Trent come from? Margaret wondered. Seemingly, he had appeared out of nowhere. She noted that Trent had changed since this morning and wore a coat of dark superfine over buckskin trousers. The coat was well cut and emphasized the width of his shoulders, and his boots were glossy with polish. He had the aspect of a man who had come courting.

"What's the matter?" he was asking. "Did that beastly woman abuse you again?"

When Margaret stood, mute, Trent shut the door of the picture gallery behind him and walked over to her. "What's the matter, Margaret?"

He didn't even notice his slip, but her heart picked up the way he had spoken her name. Eyes, green as summer leaves, looked deep into hers. "Tell me what's wrong," he pleaded.

Despising herself for the hen-hearted way she was feeling, Margaret said, "I was trying to decide how to address you."

"To *address* me?"

"*My lord* may be somewhat premature since you have not yet publically assumed your title," she said coldly, "so I suppose *Mr. Trenton* would be more appropriate."

"Hell and the devil," Trent groaned. Somewhat guiltily he added, "She told you."

"Miss Jerryham was kind enough to inform me about your elevation in the world."

"My eleva—oh, for God's sake, *don't*."

"Don't what?"

"Don't look at me like that, as if you'd like to rip me up one side and down the other," Trent growled.

Margaret turned her head away. "Then I won't look at you at all, sir."

For answer, he caught her by the shoulders and swung her about to face him. "I'm not sir to you and never have been. I thought that we were friends."

Her lower lip had begun to tremble. To counter this weakness, she glared at him. "Friends are honest with each other."

He was silent. In spite of her efforts, some of her anger dissipated when she saw the unhappy look in his eyes. "Why didn't you tell me?" she whispered.

"I started to, the day we went riding in the curricle, but then I thought it would do no good. I'm not going to inherit that beastly money for months, and I could do nothing to help you or your mother." Lamely he added, "I'm sorry."

His touch was disconcerting. The warmth of his hands seemed to reach through the thin stuff of her dress, through her skin and into her heart. Margaret knew she should shake herself free but could not bear to lose the contact with him.

She said in a low voice, "You didn't even tell me about your engagement."

"I tell you, I'm sor—*what* did you say?" Trent demanded. "Did Miss Jerryham tell you we were engaged?"

"Aren't you?"

"No!" he exclaimed, then stopped in some confusion.

"But you intend to declare yourself," Margaret pointed out.

Disturbed as he was, Trent did not hear the pain in her voice. "Well," he began, "I'd thought . . ."

"I collect that you needed prospects before you were acceptable to her parents. As you are an earl, there is nothing to be said except to wish you happy."

She smiled as she spoke, but the smile did not reach her eyes. She looked so pale, Trent thought, that the freckles stood out across the bridge of her small nose. The shadows under her eyes were like bruises. He suddenly had the insane desire to kiss away those dark smudges.

His confused emotions made him testy. "Your wishes are premature. I'm not engaged to Miss Jerryham."

Margaret's eyes turned even colder, and Trent reminded himself that he had done nothing wrong. He had wanted Miss Jerryham to be Margaret's friend, to champion her against her employer. How was he to know that she would make matters worse?

Trying to excuse Lavinia and himself, he said, "Miss Jerryham meant for the best. She must have felt that having Longmarsh for a friend would lift your spirits."

"My spirits are exceedingly high," Margaret retorted. Wishing that she could box his noble ears, she added, "I beg you will not concern yourself with me, sir."

At her icy tone, he stiffened. He'd never known Margaret could be so tongue-valiant.

"Very well, madam, if that's your wish, I will not afflict you with my presence."

Both turned their backs and took several steps in opposite directions. Then, almost in unison, they turned and stared at each other with unhappy eyes.

Trent shook his head and spoke in a dazed tone, "Hell and the devil, this won't do. We can't leave it like this. Margaret, I—"

The door of the picture gallery creaked as it swung open. "There you are, Mr. Trenton," Lavinia caroled.

Ignoring the fact that both Trent and Margaret had gone as still as the marble and bronze statues that stood along the gallery wall, Lavinia entered the dim gallery and walked languidly toward Trent.

"I learned that you had come here with Mr. Block. I have been looking everywhere for you."

Margaret noted the arch way Lavinia looked up at Trent and the befuddlement with which he gazed down at her. She couldn't blame him. Miss Jerryham was enough to turn any man's head.

She had changed for dinner into a gown of creamy lace over a pale blue satin underskirt. The dress was cut low enough to display the beginning swell of Lavinia's white bosom. A necklace of sapphires glittered on that white bosom, and diamonds glinted in her shell-pink ears.

As though she felt Margaret's eyes on her, Lavinia turned. Her eyes grew hard, as hard as her jewels. Pointedly, she turned her back.

"How unkind not to let me know you were here," she told Trent.

He glanced at Margaret. "Block and I were on our way to Longmarsh-on-Hill when we were summoned here."

"Surely not. *You* could not be summoned anywhere."

Again, Trent's eyes went to Margaret. "Lady Vere wanted Block to come to Vere Hall. She needed to talk to him, she said. He's with her now, and I'm waiting for him."

"Is that *all* that brought you here?" Lavinia dimpled adorably. "I vow you are cruel, sir."

Margaret felt something hard press into the small of her back and realized that she had backed into a marble statue. Her skirts rustled as she extricated herself, and the sound drew Lavinia's attention.

"Oh, are you still here?" she drawled.

It was not so much the words but the way in which they were said. Lavinia's tone was loaded with such contempt that Margaret felt as though she'd been slapped.

"Do go away," Lavinia begged languidly. "Don't you have something to do?"

As Margaret left the picture gallery, Trent exploded, "For God's sake, Miss Jerryham!" He turned to follow Margaret and felt Lavinia's hand on his arm.

"Let her go," Lavinia said.

He swung about to face her. "What on earth made you talk to her like that?"

Lavinia frowned. "I vow that you are acting very oddly. She *is* a paid companion, a servant, as it were."

Through his teeth Trent said, "Miss Hannay is a lady—and my friend."

Lavinia gave an enchanting trill of laughter, but her eyes had begun to sparkle dangerously. "How diverting. It sounds as if you have developed a *tendre* for this *lady*."

While she spoke, he studied her face. That face was as beautiful as ever, and yet Trent was suddenly conscious of feeling chilled. Had there always been such malice in Lavinia's expression?

But the malice was gone instantly, and clasping her hands around his arm, Lavinia coaxed, "I came to ask you if you had received Lady

Vere's invitation to her ball. If you do not stop frowning, I will not save you any of my dances."

He knew that it was his cue to protest, to beg. Lavinia Jerryham was used to entreaty from her admirers. Once Trent had played this game and even enjoyed it, but now it seemed foolish and artificial.

"If you'll excuse me," he said curtly, "I must leave you now."

Lavinia now realized that she might have been foolish to attack Margaret Hannay. She clasped Trent's arm even more firmly. "Let us not break straws," she cooed. "Indeed, if you look at me so fiercely, you will put me in a quake. Let us have a cose, like old friends."

She turned the full battery of her eyes on him, but Trent remained unmoved.

"Unfortunately, I must leave you. Block and I have business at Longmarsh-on-Hill. Wickwell's son is still ailing, you see." He extricated his arm and added curtly, "I wish you good evening, Miss Jerryham."

After he had gone, Lavinia remained where she was for some time. This Kenneth Trenton was certainly different from the young man who had courted her last season. Then, he had dogged her footsteps, had hung on every word, had languished for her notice. Now, her charms had no effect on him.

She had always liked the handsome young man, but he had seemed cut from the same cloth as her many other gallants. Now he was stronger, surer, harder. Even without the added attraction of a title, Kenneth Trenton was most definitely interesting.

Lavinia caught her underlip in her teeth. Then, recalling that gnawing her lip might spoil its perfection, she composed herself and tilted her chin.

She meant to have the new Earl of Longmarsh, and no encroaching servant was going to stand in her way.

"Can you guess what Lady Vere asked me?" Block wanted to know.

It was half an hour later, and the land steward's landaulet was rolling sedately toward Longmarsh-on-Hill. The journey up till now had been a silent one, for Block seemed preoccupied with his own thoughts and Trent's mind was in turmoil.

He desperately needed to talk to Margaret. As soon as he had left the picture gallery, he had tried to find her, but Vere Hall seemed to have swallowed her up, and none of the servants had been able to help.

Trent didn't blame Margaret for being angry. He still found it hard to believe that Lavinia had given Margaret such a nasty setdown. When he thought of how Margaret must be feeling . . .

"What do you think, my lord?" Block was asking.

Trent realized that the land steward had been talking for some time. He temporized, "I'm not quite sure."

"Nor am I certain," Block agreed. "I fail to see why Lady Vere would need to know Longmarsh's worth."

Trent jerked around and stared at his companion. "She asked you about the estate's finances?"

Block nodded and pursed his lips. "The reason given by her ladyship," he said unctuously, "was that a nephew of hers is dissatisfied with the revenues produced by his land. She desired me—oh, very courteously—to tell her what 'an estate like Longmarsh' could produce in a year. As a basis of, ah, comparison, so to speak."

"What did you tell her?"

"I explained that I could not hope to be, ah, accurate without my ledgers. For a moment I almost thought that she would ask me to bring them, but she contented herself by asking me several pointed questions about, ah, Longmarsh's revenues. She professed herself astonished."

Trent could well believe this. He had learned enough about his future estate to realize its wealth in wool and livestock as well.

"I've never seen a more efficiently run place," he mused. "I remember one friend at school whose people owned property in the south. Braitherwell, his name was. He invited me down one holiday, and it was a ramshackle place, going all to weed. And the tenants! Muffin-faced, complaining duffers, all of them. There's nothing like that here."

Block nodded. "Your great-uncle prided himself on his attention to detail. He felt that tenants were, ah, the backbone of his estate, and he treated everyone as fairly as he wished himself to be treated. He knew every man, woman, and child by name."

But Trent's mind was otherwise occupied. "I'll wager you that Lady Vere doesn't have a nephew. What's her real reason for wanting to know about Longmarsh, I wonder?"

Block gave a deprecating little cough. "I venture to say, sir, that, ah, it is not Lady Vere who is interested in the revenue of your future estate. Lady Jerryham was also present at the interview. If I might make so bold, Lady Jerryham has a much more, ah, vested interest in Longmarsh."

Trent narrowed his eyes.

"There is perhaps the possibility," Block said delicately, "that you will, ah, be connected to her family. Lady Vere hinted that it is your, ah, intention to offer for Miss Jerryham."

Their arrival in the village saved Trent from reacting to this. "There's Wickwell now!" he exclaimed.

A squat little man with a square, sunburned face came hurrying toward them. "How is your boy, Joseph?" Block asked. "Better, I trust?"

In spite of his own problems, Trent was moved by the hunted expression in the father's eyes. "No, sir, our Sam's mighty poorly. We dunno know what can be done for him—he can hardly catch his breath. The missus an' me are worrit out o' our minds."

Trent followed the land agent into a small cottage nearby. As soon as he walked through the door, he heard the sick child's labored breathing. Trent greeted Mrs. Wickwell and then went to stand by the small bed. The poor little blighter did look much worse, he thought.

"Hullo, Sam," he said bracingly.

The lad did his best to smile, and seeing that smile, Trent felt something twist in his chest.

He was astonished. He hadn't known the Wickwells for very long, and in any case they were humble people with whom a gentleman would not usually involve himself. But as he looked from the sick child to his mother, Trent remembered how worried Margaret had been about Elsie Culp. Perhaps because he was thinking of her so much, he couldn't help seeing the Wickwells through Margaret's eyes.

"Has the doctor been called in, Mrs. Wickwell?" he asked abruptly. "When we came here last, you said there was a sawbones at Harton-on-Wold."

The woman shook her head. "Doctor wouldn't see Sam, sir."

"He wouldn't? Why not? It's his business, isn't it, to see sick people?"

Wickwell said heavily, "I got the trap and took Sam and th' missus out to Harton-on-Wold to see 'un, and he said—"

"He sent us packing," Mrs. Wickwell interrupted bitterly. "Now that there's the mineral spring, there's gentry coming to Harton-on-Wold. Doctor didn't want his important patients catching anything nasty from Sam."

"We'll see about that," Trent exclaimed wrathfully. He turned to Block, adding. "I'm going to take the landaulet and drive Mrs. Wickwell and the boy to see the sawbones."

Wickwell looked surprised at Trent's masterful tone. He glanced uncertainly at Block, but the land agent only nodded. "Certainly," he agreed. "That is, ah, the best course of action."

Mrs. Wickwell lost no time in bundling up her

son. Then a thought occurred to her. "But supposing the doctor won't see us?"

"You let me worry about that," Trent said.

It was much later—after dark, in fact—before Trent returned with a sleeping Sam and an exhausted but grateful Mrs. Wickwell. It took some time to settle the child and even longer to compose the weeping mother, who called down every imaginable blessing on Mr. Trenton's head. On the way back to his cottage, Trent explained what had happened.

"That damned doctor didn't want to treat young Sam. Reasoning with the man didn't do any good, so I told him if he didn't hop to it, I'd horsewhip him. And *of course* the child didn't have anything that the right medicine couldn't cure. He feels better already."

Trent reflected a moment. "Why is there no village doctor, Block? I can't understand what my great-uncle was thinking, leaving those people at the mercy of that pompous quack. Oh, you say the old doctor died? Time, then, to get ahold of a new one. Quickly, too."

Looking very smug about something, the land agent agreed. Just then Trent heard the sound of running water above the clip-clop of the horses' hooves. They were at the trout stream near the copse of trees where he had first met Margaret.

He was immediately reminded of his personal problems. "I'll leave you here," he said abruptly, and, swinging down from the landaulet, strode down the road toward the Hannays' tumbledown cottage.

Mrs. Link met him at the door and looked surprised to see him. "Mrs. Hannay's resting, sir," she explained. "Miss Margaret? No, she's not home yet. Probably still working at the hall," she added darkly. "Since those Lunnon guests came to visit, Lady Vere's been a reg'lar tartar. My boy says poor Miss Margaret don't have a minute to herself."

Trent walked down the steps and stood wondering what to do next. He admitted that he hadn't the faintest idea of how to proceed. Should he ride back to Vere Hall and demand to speak to Margaret? No, that would not do.

"She'll think I came to see Lavinia," Trent muttered.

He thought of the goddess he had adored for so long and remembered the artifice of her fluttering eyelashes, the tap of her fan, her practiced smile. He thought of Lady Jerryham attempting to assess Longmarsh's financial worth. Had he actually loved Lavinia? Perhaps. Or perhaps he had been so caught up in the atmosphere of the Season that he had been bedazzled by her beauty. Trent tried to picture Lavinia at the Wickwell's this evening and saw her pulling back her skirts to avoid contagion.

"No thank you," he said aloud.

Margaret had no art, no pretence. She was simply herself. Pluck to the backbone, warm, and true—that was Margaret. A vivid beauty, with a spirit to match and a ready laugh—that was Margaret also. And today they had parted in anger.

There was the sound of twigs snapping underfoot, and Trent's heart bounded with relief. Margaret was walking down the path toward the cottage. She was alone, and in spite of the darkness she moved with her distinctive, free stride.

She wasn't aware of him until he took a step toward her. Then she stopped and put a hand up to her throat. "Who is there?" she asked uncertainly.

She looked so lovely in the twilight that he had to clear his throat before he could reply. "It's Trent."

In spite of the darkness he could sense her stiffen. The hand at her throat was lowered slowly to her side. "Did you lose your way?" she asked coldly.

He took a step toward her and she immediately took one backward. "Perhaps I did lose my way in a manner of speaking. Miss Hannay, I need to explain—"

"I assure you that I understand fully."

She started to walk past him. He attempted to take her hand, but she eluded his grasp. The door to the cottage swung open and Mrs. Link peered outside suspiciously.

"Good night, my lord," Margaret said.

He pleaded, "I've made a mull of things. I know that, and I am sorry for it. I'll do anything you say, if you'd only listen to me."

Without a backward look, she stepped toward the door.

"Hang it," Trent roared. "Margaret, come back! Will you listen to me?"

The door banged shut on his words.

Chapter Nine

Lavinia smiled at her plump and perspiring partner. "That is most interesting, Mr. Montesque," she purred. "Pray, tell me more."

Montesque wanted to oblige but couldn't. His brain-box, he was the first to admit, was not at its best. The ordeal of staying at Norsby had left him a mere shadow of himself. Also, the buckram padding in the shoulders of his bottle-green coat and the corset that nipped in his waist were causing him the torments of the damned.

And here was the beauteous Miss Jerryham dancing the cotillion with him and hanging on his every word. It was a heady experience, something that always seemed to happen to other fellows but had never happened to him. Desperately wanting to come up to snuff, Montesque affected an attitude of *savoir-faire*.

Lavinia thought he looked like a pop-eyed trout.

"I collect that you and the earl—I mean, Mr. Trenton, are best friends, is that not so?" she cooed.

Tonight Lavinia looked more than usually divine in a blue silk slip with a silvery gauze overdress. Her long sleeves were caught up by pearls, and more pearls, sapphires, and tiny white roses were wreathed through her golden hair. Small feet in blue satin slippers embroidered with roses tapped out the measure of the dance. She was the most exquisite creature Montesque had ever seen, and he had to remind himself quite sharply that he was dancing with Trent's beloved. Poaching on a friend's preserves was definitely not ton.

"Yes, we're friends," he stammered. "Devoted, give you my word."

"And you and Mr. Butterworth were there when he was first told of his great-uncle's will? That is *so* interesting."

Montesque cleared his throat. "Thought Trent was coming to the ball tonight."

Lavinia's alabaster forehead wrinkled in a frown. "He is late."

Lady Vere's ball had been a success so far. Whatever his shortcomings, Barnaby had performed a miracle. Under his direction the gloomy cavern of the great hall had been transformed into a scene out of a fairy tale. The dusty ancestral hangings and the rusting weaponry had vanished. In their place were gleaming silver sconces and hanging baskets of hothouse flowers. The formidable Jacobean chairs had been wreathed with more flowers and had been positioned so that chaperones could observe their young charges dancing.

The orchestra's tireless playing caused the scented air to vibrate with music, and the sound of dancing rose over the talk and laughter of Lady Vere's guests. Some of these, like the Jerryhams and the Honorable Vincent Federby, were houseguests. Others had arrived lately. Ladies in muslins, silks, and satins fluttered like birds of paradise; equally gorgeous gentlemen in bright coats, flowered waistcoats, and fashionably skintight breeches escorted them.

More ladies and gentlemen were constantly entering the great hall, but though Lavinia kept glancing hopefully at the door, there was no sign of Kenneth Trenton, new earl of Longmarsh.

That was most aggravating, but it was not the worst she had to endure. It set Lavinia's teeth on edge to see that, due to some caprice of Lady Vere's, the Hannay creature was also present.

No doubt Lady Vere had sought to humiliate her paid companion by setting her shabbiness against the finery of the other guests. In this she had failed. Though Margaret was dressed in a plain green crêpe gown that had seen better days, and though her white neck and shoulders were bare of ornament, she still looked as fresh and as lovely as the rose in her hair.

Aware of Lavinia's hostile gaze, Margaret kept her attention centered on Jermyn Butterworth, who for the past ten minutes had been recounting the story of how Mr. Brummell had insulted the Prince Regent.

"They had been on the outs for some time, and of course it was Prinny's fault for cutting Brummell to start with," Button was explaining, "not the thing at all, the cut direct. Actually, Miss Hannay," Button added as an aside, "Prinny did look ludicrous that night. He might consider himself Prince Florizel, but, don't you know, those days are over and done with. What with the corsets the man wears, how can he appear to be a romantic figure?" He paused and wondered, "Where was I?"

"The Prince Regent and Mr. Brummell were at Lord Alvanley's ball," Margaret prompted.

Button was grateful. He had become quite fond of Miss Hannay. She didn't interrupt or yawn or laugh in the wrong places. She actually *listened* to a fellow.

"Well," he recommenced, "Prinny went up to talk to his host, but he cut Brummell, who was standing beside Alvanley. Brummell was furious, but he didn't show it. He said in a carrying tone, 'Alvanley, who is your fat friend?' "

Margaret was shocked. "What did the prince do?"

"He turned scarlet and then very pale. I am sure he gnashed his teeth." Button had thought that everyone had heard this old chestnut by now, and Margaret's unfeigned interest was very gratifying. A very nice lady, he thought, and actually quite stylish. In her simple dress and with that rose in her hair, she somehow made every other woman in the room looked overdressed. A pity this wasn't London, or she might set a new style.

He wondered if he should invite Miss Hannay to dance but decided against it. It wasn't because she was a mere lady's companion. He hoped he was too much of a gentleman to regard such things, but the orchestra had started a Scottish reel, and the idea of cutting figure eights and doing innumerable *pas de bas* fatigued him. Besides, though many guests were going through the vigorous steps, just as many were standing or sitting to watch the dancers.

Button regarded these onlookers through his quizzing glass. There was Lady Jerryham queening it over the local gentry while her brother drank steadily in a corner; there was Lady Vere talking to a dumpy little woman and an elderly man in regimentals; and over there was Miss Adela Lakehart peeping coquettishly at him over her fan.

If he danced with Miss Hannay, he would, in politeness, have to stand up with Miss Lakehart as well. Button shuddered, thinking that he had endured much for friendship's sake. During the past few weeks he had been plagued by Miss Lakehart, pursued by Miss Lakehart, and forced to escort Miss Lakehart everywhere. Perhaps Monty would stand up with Miss Hannay? But Monty was hopping about with Miss Lavinia Jerryham.

"I wonder where Trent is," he remarked idly. "Lady Vere expressly said that he was invited, so we assumed that all had been revealed, don't you know, and his disguise had been penetrated. I thought he'd be here by the time we arrived."

"I am sure that he will arrive presently," Margaret said, then added, "Will you excuse me? Lady Vere is signaling that she wishes to speak to me."

She didn't care where Trent was. She had not the slightest interest in his whereabouts or in whether she ever set eyes on him again.

The only person who would see him was Mrs. Hannay. "The dear boy really came to talk to you, Margaret," that distressed lady had said, "and when I explained that you would not see him, he looked most unhappy. Really, dear one, are you *quite* sure about what you are doing? Trent is such a pleasant young man, and Mrs.

Link assures me that the people of the village have lost their hearts to him." Mrs. Hannay had paused to add wistfully, "And I miss his visits."

Margaret could not reveal Trent's secret even to her mother, nor could she describe that scene in the picture gallery. Even thinking about it hurt.

She became aware that Lady Vere was talking to her. "This is Colonel Bracey and Mrs. Bracey. They wished to meet you since the colonel knew your father."

Putting Trent firmly from her mind, Margaret curtsied to the elderly couple before her. The motherly lady smiled; the gentleman, who sported an enormous, graying handlebar mustache, bowed a very proper, very military bow.

"Your father was Captain Percival Hannay of the dragoon guards? What? I had the honor of serving with him, ma'am," he rumbled.

Margaret's eyes brightened. "Indeed, sir, he often spoke of a Colonel Horatio Bracey, an officer for whom he had the highest regard."

The colonel tweaked his mustache and cleared his throat several times. "Finer officer never lived," he said at last. "Pity he sold his colors. What? Loss to the guards. Now, Miss Hannay, my good lady and I took the liberty of calling on your mother this afternoon to express our deepest sympathies. I was telling Lady Vere how much we enjoyed meeting Mrs. Hannay."

"That is so true. We spent a delightful hour with your dear mama," Mrs. Bracey put in. She smiled and took Margaret's hands, adding, "Forgive us, my dear, for not making ourselves known to you at once. We did not know you were Captain Hannay's daughter. When we learned the truth from Lady Vere, you were otherwise occupied. However, we sought out Mrs. Hannay without delay."

She turned to her hostess as she spoke, but Lady Vere was no longer there. She was sailing down the great hall to greet a new arrival. "Oh, Mr. er, Trenton," she was gushing, "it is so good of you to have come."

Margaret was determined not to look in Trent's direction. She gazed fixedly at a garland of roses that decorated the wall ahead of her and made polite conversation with Colonel Bracey and his wife. She was priding herself on her cool behavior when she heard Trent's voice.

"I'm sorry to be late, ma'am. There was a matter that needed clearing up in the village. A dispute between two families that needed to be settled."

Margaret clenched her hands. It wasn't fair, she thought bitterly, that Trent should have the kind of voice that cut through music and laughter and reached out to her in an almost physical way. *I'm not going to look at him,* she reminded herself.

"Of course. The old earl was always so conscientious about his tenants," Lady Vere gushed.

Margaret couldn't resist glancing at her employer. Her toadeating ladyship looked as though butter wouldn't melt in her mouth. Her eyes were fixed worshipfully on Trent's face. Her smile showed all of her teeth. Remembering the first time the two had met, Margaret wanted to laugh.

Mrs. Bracey's keen eyes had followed Margaret's glance. "What a handsome young man!" she exclaimed. "Do you know who he is, Miss Hannay?"

"He is Mr. Kenneth Trenton of London," Margaret said, and stopped short. Naming him was a mistake. Slowly, inexorably, she found her head turning back to the spot where Trent stood.

He had never looked so handsome. His black evening coat was simply but skillfully cut, as were his white waistcoat and dark breeches. They set off to perfection Trent's broad shoulders and the muscles of his thighs and legs.

Green eyes in a tanned face glowed as they met hers, and Margaret felt as though she had fallen a hundred feet. She attempted to catch her breath and failed dismally. There was a dull roaring in her ears.

The careful logic that had supported her now collapsed like a house of cards. I've missed him so much, Margaret thought.

Involuntarily, she took a half step toward him. Trent saw the movement. His heart, which had felt like a lead weight for the past few days, suddenly soared over the moon.

He realized that Lady Vere was tapping his arm with her fan. "Your attention is wandering, sir," she said archly. "I don't wonder at it. The lady is *very* lovely."

"Very lovely, indeed," Trent agreed fervently.

Lady Vere beamed. She envisioned telling all and sundry that she had not only been the first to invite the Earl of Longmarsh to her ball but had overseen the details of his betrothal. And, naturally, Alice Jerryham would be most grateful.

Her ladyship preened herself. Her connection

with the Jerryhams and thus to the Earl of Long-marsh would give her the entrée into the most high-in-the-instep houses in London. She would be invited *everywhere*.

"You must not stand on ceremony," she tittered. "Go and dance with her at once, my lord—if I may be the first to call you that?"

Trent had no idea at all what the old griffin was babbling about. For him the great hall had emptied of all save one woman. She looked like springtime, he thought, in that leaf-green dress with the single rose in her hair.

Leaving Lady Vere talking to herself, he strode over to Margaret. As his intention became clear, his hostess's smile froze on her lips. Lavinia, who had been dancing spiritedly, suddenly missed a step and landed on Montesque's foot.

Trent was unaware of either event. He had come to a stop in front of Margaret and had realized, suddenly, that he didn't know what to say.

He was no stranger to polite society. He was always at ease at the opera, at Almack's, at house parties and routs and balls. He had squired debs, reigning beauties, and dashing young widows as well as less respectable but far more interesting damsels. Now, suddenly, he felt like a tongue-tied schoolboy with two left feet. His usual aplomb and practiced grace took French leave, and he could only gaze mutely at Margaret.

There was something the matter with her tongue, Margaret decided. When she opened her lips, the polite setdown she'd intended to give to Mr. Kenneth Trenton disappeared, and all that came out was a hen-hearted gasp.

A rumbling cough reminded her of the Braceys, and she turned to them almost desperately.

"Mrs. Bracey, C-Colonel, may I pre-present Mr. Kenneth Trenton," she stammered.

Trent bowed in a bemused way, and the colonel concealed a smile beneath his mustache. "Servant, Mr. Trenton," he rumbled, then added significantly, "ah, they're playing a waltz. Romantic dance, the waltz. What? Come, my dear, we must attempt it. Dum-dum-dum-da . . ."

Humming pointedly, he propelled his wife away. Young love must be served, the colonel thought benevolently. Then he exclaimed, "By gad! I beg your pardon!" as a very beautiful young lady almost collided with him.

Lavinia didn't hear the colonel. She certainly didn't see him. Her eyes were fixed on Kenneth Trenton, who was gazing into the Hannay creature's upturned face.

"Miss Hannay," Trent was asking, "will you do me the honor of waltzing with me?"

"But of course I will," Lavinia cried.

She shouldered Margaret aside and smiled up into Trent's eyes. "You are late," she purred. "I was persuaded you had forgotten to come."

She placed her beringed white hand on his arm and, totally ignoring Margaret, began to walk toward the dancers. She walked alone. Trent stepped backward, letting Lavinia's hand slide off his arm.

"Miss Hannay," he repeated, "will you honor me?"

It seemed to Margaret that everything whirled around her. For a second she was aware of Lavinia's fury, of Lady Vere's shock, of George Montesque and Jermyn Butterworth staring. Then a demon of recklessness seized her, and she curtsied almost to the floor. "I would be most pleased, Mr. Trenton," she said. "I love to waltz."

His bow would have flattered a queen, and he offered his arm to her as if she were an empress. In a trance, Margaret touched her fingers to the sleeve of his coat and swept past Lavinia. As Trent whirled her into the dance, she hardly felt the ground beneath her feet.

It seemed to Trent that Margaret's beauty was incandescent. It was as though some light within her made her glow. But, as they dipped and swayed, he saw that brilliance begin to dim.

"Don't," he begged her earnestly.

She didn't pretend to misunderstand him. "But you snubbed Miss Jerryham by asking me to dance. She's your fiancée, Mr. Trenton."

"No, she's not. I never asked her to marry me. That was all in her head. And I'm not *Mr.* anything. I'm Trent."

Her eyes had stars reflected in them. "You told me that before," she said breathlessly. "And I said 'Miss Hannay will not do, either.' Do you remember?"

"I love you," Trent told her.

So this, Margaret reflected dreamily, was what it felt like. It began with a melting in one's limbs and then one's blood began to dance and skip like bubbles of champagne.

What was the use of trying to escape from the truth? It had been standing at her shoulder all these lonely days when she had avoided Trent. It had stalked her tonight as she watched Lavinia preen herself for the ball. Then, she had felt hollow, emptied of everything that mattered. Now, she was renewed with joy.

With great presence of mind, Trent had danced toward the French windows at the far end of the great hall. Now he whisked Margaret through them and into the darkness beyond. He waltzed her down the path toward the topiary garden and up to a bed of roses. Here he stopped.

"My dear love," the Earl of Longmarsh whispered.

As she raised her mouth for Trent's kiss, Margaret was aware of a slight rustling in the rosebushes nearby. She paid no attention. Brain, heart, and soul were intent on kissing and being kissed. Her hands stroked Trent's hard jaw, worked upward to his hair. The crisp curls wound themselves around her fingers as if they, too, adored her.

"Will you marry me?" Trent asked between kisses. "You'd better. I'll haunt you till you do. I'll camp on your doorstep and— God, what nonsense I'm talking. Marry me, Margaret."

He kissed her eyes, the tip of her nose, her temples, her chin. He stroked her lovely hair. He couldn't get enough of holding her in his arms.

Finally, sheer want of breath drove them apart. Keeping his arms around her as though afraid she might disappear, Trent looked down into her lovely, uptilted, smiling face.

"Well, dear one?" he asked shakily.

It seemed as though the night were stocked with shooting stars, comets, and moons. Margaret wanted to jump up and down and shout "Hooray!" Instead, she raised her kiss-rosy lips to his again.

"Dearest Trent," she whispered, "I have been in love with you for so long. Don't you know that?"

"And *then*?" Nancy demanded. "Don't you stop there, you little demon, or I'll pull yer ears. What happened?"

Noah grinned at the anxious faces that ringed him. He hopped nimbly aside, evading Nancy's grasp. "Wot do you fink 'appened?"

Link's fingers curled as though they, too, itched to pull Noah's ears. "Little perisher," he snarled.

Noah's grin widened. They were all dying to know whether Miss Margaret had accepted Mr. Trenton, and he, by dint of hiding in the prickly rosebushes, was the only one who could supply the answer.

"I needs somefing to eat," he announced.

"Wot you will get is a boot up yer backside," the cook threatened. But she slapped down a plate loaded with bread, butter, and—Noah's eyes widened—slices of cold beef. He reached for this unexpected largesse, but Nancy snatched the plate away.

"Not till you tells us what happened."

The pot-boy pretended to hesitate. He had never before been the focus of so much attention, and he felt a heady sense of power.

"It were pretty dark under them bushes," he hedged. "Prickly, too. Nasty things was crawling all over me feet." His audience nodded. "Mr. Trenton asked Miss Margaret to marry 'im, like

I said." More nods. "And then ... Ain't there any more beef, Cook?"

"If you don't tell us what yer know, I'll put *you* in me stew," the cook shrieked.

Elsie said scornfully, "I bet he didn't see nothing. I bet he's making it up."

"Little liar," Link added.

Insulted, Noah shouted, "Seen them kissing, didn't I? 'Eard Mr. Trenton telling Miss that he wanted to tell 'er 'e loved 'er afore this, but that short o' shooting Lady Vere there weren't nofing 'e could 'ave done to help 'er. But now, Mr. Trent says, Miss and 'er ma must leave 'er leddyship and go to 'is people in Surrey where 'is mùm 'ud take care o' them proper."

Noah attempted to deepen his tone. " 'You'll give yer notice this very night,' 'e says, 'an' to 'ell wi' Lady Vere.' Then 'e tells Miss Margaret that 'e'd see 'er ma in the morning to ask fer 'er 'and. An' *she* says what if 'is ma don't like 'er? An' *e* says, 'You're too beautiful to talk gammon. My mother will adore you.' Then they kissed some more, and—"

"Cease and desist immediately!"

Noah stopped in midsentence. Reddington and Mrs. Pollyshot were walking into the servants' hall. The floorboards shook at the weight of their combined approach.

"Wicked boy," the butler roared. "How dare you eavesdrop on your betters?"

Noah's erstwhile audience took several steps away from him. Seeing that he stood alone, the pot-boy's courage ebbed. "I meant no 'arm," he whined.

"You are a disgrace to the household! You shall

be dismissed without a character! You will end your days in the workhouse or in prison!"

Noah looked about him for support, found none, and began to blubber. "I wanted to 'ear the music and the dancing," he wailed. "Looked so pretty the ladies did, and the gentry were all puffed up like peacocks. And Miss Margaret—when she came frew the door in 'is arms, she looked like I ain't never seen 'er, like a princess she were—"

"She's in love," Nancy said. Her eyes were soft and faraway. "She's been in love with Mr. Trent for ages."

Link had begun to smile all over his face at the thought of Miss Margaret settled and happy and out of Lady Vere's clutches.

Reddington felt that he should say something to dam the staff's enthusiasm, especially since it resulted from the abominable Noah's eavesdropping, but Mrs. Pollyshot forestalled him.

"What else did you overhear?" she asked Noah. "Speak up sharp, and no lies."

"Mr. Trenton's going to be an h'earl," Noah said, snivelling.

He screamed when Reddington's great paw descended and seized him by the ear. Elevating the pot-boy several inches off the floor, Reddington demanded in awful tones, "*What* did you say?"

"Lawks, an h'earl!" Mrs. Pollyshot cried, forgetting her diction in her excitement. "Mr. Trenton an h'earl! Ooh, I never did. I feel faint."

In mortal fear as well as in pain, Noah yelled, " 'E's going to be the new h'earl of Longmarsh!"

"God bless my soul," Reddington gasped. He

dropped Noah back to earth. "God bless my soul!" he repeated. "I cannot credit—"

But Nancy's joyful scream interrupted him. "That means Miss Margaret's going to be a *countess*!"

She caught Elsie around the waist, and they began to jig about. In a moment, Link joined them, then the cook. Mrs. Pollyshot clapped her hands to her heart. Noah began to beat his spoon on the table while at the same time stuffing his mouth with food.

Reddington scowled, but even this did nothing to spoil the general jubilation.

" 'Ooray!" Noah shouted with his mouth full. " 'Ooray fer Miss Margaret what's going ter marry an h'earl. 'Ooray!"

In the early hours of the morning Lady Vere's ball began to wind down. Neighbors summoned their carriages preparatory to going home, while the exhausted houseguests sought their rooms. The Honorable Vincent Federby, who had indulged too heavily in claret Latiffe and brandy, called for his valet and the chamberpot. Link and the other footmen had their work cut out for them as they oversaw departing carriages and attended to the male houseguests while Nancy and Elsie flew to do the bidding of the various ladies.

Whether that task was light or difficult depended on the guest. Mrs. Bracey, the colonel's wife, was a matter-of-fact person content with being served by her own abigail, but Lady Jerryham was another matter.

"Fit to be tied she is, and it's little wonder," Nancy said, grinning to Elsie when they met for an instant on the landing. "Nothing's going to please *her* tonight. She thought that—Mr. Trenton was going to offer for her daughter, she did."

"The mistress's not happy, neither." Elsie sighed, for her ear was ringing from a slap from that lady. "I never did see her in such a mood before. White with temper she is."

In fact, Lady Jerryham had just spent a tense five minutes with her hostess, an interview that left Lady Vere shaking with rage. When Elsie had popped her face around the door in answer to a violent summons, she had been called clumsy and slow and slapped for her pains.

"Go fetch Miss Hannay at once, you little fool. Be quick about it," Lady Vere had snarled.

A good thing that Miss didn't have to play up to her ladyship anymore, Elsie thought as she hastened to carry out her orders.

Required by her employer to stay the night at Vere Hall, Margaret was in the small room on the third floor. When Elsie knocked, she was still dressed.

Elsie had never seen Miss Margaret look so radiant before. Quite forgetting Lady Vere's message, she clasped her hands and cried, "Oh, miss, we all wishes you happy, I'm sure."

"Wish me— How did you know?" Margaret exclaimed. Then she hugged Elsie and added, "Never mind. It doesn't matter. Oh, dear Elsie, I'm so happy I could jump over the moon."

"Yes, ma'am." Elsie beamed all over her small, homely face. "I'm that glad as Mr. Trenton ain't a groom nor yet a land steward assistant but is going to be an earl."

"And it was supposed to be a secret." Margaret's eyes danced. "I *heard* something rustling in the rosebushes. Was it Noah?"

Elsie described the scene in the servants' hall. "We was all struck dumb. Even Mr. Reddington didn't have nofing to say. And then, Mrs. Pollyshot, she said as she knew that Mr. Trenton was going to be a bang-up earl acourse he do care about his tenants and people are saying good things about him in the village. Me mam says so, too." Suddenly she paused, her eyes widening. "Lawks, I forgot. Mistress wants to see you, miss. And she's ever so cross."

Margaret's joy was suddenly checked. She had known that her employer would demand an account of her actions at the ball, but she had hoped that this one night, at least, would pass in perfect happiness.

"I'd best go to her now." She sighed.

"Yes, miss," Elsie agreed sympathetically. "I'm sorry."

Margaret walked across the landing to Lady Vere's bedchamber. Her ladyship's sour-faced dresser, Palley, bared her teeth when she answered Margaret's knock.

"Oh," she said rudely, "it's you." And then she smiled.

The smile boded ill. Inwardly marshaling her defenses, Margaret walked into my lady's domain. "Ma'am," she said, and waited.

Lady Vere, seated at her dressing table, glared at her companion. She flicked a hand, dismissing Palley. When that disappointed individual had left, she spoke in a hissing whisper. "You slut!"

Margaret felt her blood drain away. Anger

such as she had never before known shook her. She did not recognize her own voice when she said, "I beg your pardon?"

"You will never have my pardon. I took you in when you had nothing. Who are you? A pauper forced to earn your bread. You and your sickly mother have nothing, *are* nothing! And yet you dare to act the harlot under my roof."

Margaret gripped the back of a chair. It took all her self-control to refrain from throwing it at her employer. "Think of what you are saying, ma'am," she warned.

But her ladyship was too furious for restraint.

"You tempted young Trenton into dancing with you. Oh, I know you, miss," she went on, narrowing her gray eyes and launching each word like an arrow. "I know what kind of scheming upstart you are. You learned about his prospects and set out to have him. Well, my gel, he may have thrown his leg over you, but he'll never make you his countess."

Margaret turned her back and made for the door. "Where are you going?" Lady Vere screamed.

"To listen to you degrades us both."

Lady Vere catapulted out of her chair and raged across the room. "Do you think for one moment that he'll marry you? You're a fool if you do. You have no breeding, no morals, no money!" she hissed. "When he's tumbled you and tired of such customhouse goods as you, he'll toss you back into the gutter where you belong."

"You," Margaret interrupted, "are contemptible."

Lady Vere reared like a shying horse. Her hand

went back to deliver a slap, but Margaret caught it in midair. As her fingers closed tightly about the older woman's wrist, she spoke with deadly calm.

"I would not do that if I were you."

Furious gray eyes met steady hazel ones. After a moment, Lady Vere unwillingly looked away.

Margaret said, "You are right. I have no fortune. But my blood and my breeding is as good as yours, Lady Vere. Better, since I scruple to tell you what I think of you." She dropped her ladyship's hand as though it were something dirty.

Lady Vere panted, "You are dismissed. Without a character. Try to find another post, miss, when your gallant throws you out."

Margaret looked at the woman who had made her life a hell for the past several months and felt nothing beyond a dull disgust.

"You are an abominable woman," she said clearly. "You are vulgar and coarse. You are a bully, ma'am, who toadies to quality because you have no quality of your own."

Lady Vere had become very pale. "Get out!" she screamed.

Margaret turned to the door. The grace of her movements did not betray the fact that her legs were shaking. She looked regal, and as enraged as she was, Lady Vere felt a sudden check.

Supposing the impossible happened and young Trenton *did* make Margaret Hannay his countess? Such things had been known to occur.

Lady Vere was aware of a cold sensation at the base of her spine. If Margaret Hannay married the new earl, there would be hell to pay. She, Lady Vere, would be shunned by everyone who was anxious to toadeat for Longmarsh's favor. Doors would be closed to her everywhere. She would not be *received*.

Her ladyship made a gobbling sound in her throat. With her hand on the doorknob, Margaret turned.

"Good night, Lady Vere," she said with quiet dignity. "Pray give my excuses to Lady Jerryham and her daughter. I trust that none of us will ever meet again."

Chapter Ten

Margaret did not even pause long enough to fetch her bonnet and cloak. She could not bear to remain in Lady Vere's house for another moment.

As she hurried down the grand stairs, her legs were still trembling. When she reached the ground floor, she did not wait for a footman but pulled open the front door and went outside.

Then she paused to try to collect her thoughts. Unfamiliar emotions roiled through her. She felt revolted yet triumphant. She had finally told Lady Vere what she thought of her, but the telling left a sour taste in her mouth.

She closed her eyes and willed the vicious image of her employer to fade. Instead, she thought of strolling through the topiary garden with Trent's arm around her waist. There they had planned their future, and Trent had said . . .

"I tell you, she's gone."

Startled out of her thoughts by Montesque's voice, Margaret drew back into the shadows. Here she watched two shadowy forms come stealing out of the topiary garden.

"I've got to be certain." There was real terror in Button's drawl. "Look, Monty, be a good fellow and see if that woman isn't lurking about somewhere. I wouldn't put it past her to ambush me."

Montesque tutted. "Miss Lakehart's gone home with her parents in the landaulet. Must be thinking it particularly rag-mannered of us not to have accompanied them, give you my word. Should have gone with them, Button."

A shiver ran the length of his companion.

"You would not think so if you were the object of Adela Lakehart's attentions." He added feelingly, "If I never set eyes on Norsby again, it will be too soon."

Montesque agreed with this. "I'm fed up to my back teeth with this whole plaguey part of the world. Tell you what, Button. Let's do a bolt to London."

"London." His companion sighed.

"Yes, London. And White's and Boodles' and Brooks's." Montesque added longingly, "I haven't touched a pack of cards since we came here except to play whist and filthy silver loo. Trent's well on his way into parson's mousetrap. No point in us hanging about, is there?"

"Let me *think*, Monty."

Margaret heard the sound of heavy breathing as Mr. Jermyn Butterworth sought to marshal his thoughts.

"I'm not so sure about leaving," he finally said. "I don't know what's come over Trent. His actions tonight were dashed peculiar. Did you see the way Miss Jerryham rushed out to greet him when he arrived?" Montesque nodded. "And what did Trent do, I ask you? He left Miss Jerryham standing with her mouth open and waltzed off with Miss Hannay."

"Ah," Montesque murmured significantly.

"Not done, Monty. Not the thing at all, my dear fellow."

In the shadows, Margaret caught her lower lip between her teeth. She listened with heightened attention as Montesque agreed, "Not ton at all."

"Right in the middle of the ball, in front of everyone, don't you know." Warming to his own words, Button added, "That's not to say that Miss Hannay isn't a fine woman. Good address and very pretty. I thought that in her green dress she looked like a nymph or dryad or whatever those females were who used to hang around trees in the olden days. Or did they live in them, I wonder?"

Montesque said he didn't have the slightest idea about dryads but agreed that Miss Hannay had looked very well that evening. Suddenly he paused and added in hushed tones, "Button, you don't think . . . Trent ain't in *love* with Miss Hannay, d'you think? Can't mean to marry her!"

Audibly pained, Button begged his friend not to talk such slum. "It's out of the question, my dear fellow. An earl and a lady's companion? Naturally, such a match wouldn't fadge. Trent's not lost to *all* sense."

They moved away, still debating Trent's incomprehensible behavior. In the shadows of the house, Margaret continued to stand so still that she did not even appear to be breathing. So still was she that Link, coming to lock the doors, did not see her until the pale flutter of her dress caught his eye,

173

"Who's there?" he demanded sharply, and then exclaimed, "Miss Margaret! Wot're you doing out here wit'out yer cloak an' all?"

She did not respond, and he peered at her more closely. Her face was so white that he was startled.

"Miss, are you all right?" Link gasped.

"I am perfectly fine."

Her voice sounded different, Link thought.

"Wot has happened, miss?" She shuddered violently and he exclaimed, "You're that cold, you're frozen!"

She blinked hard and seemed suddenly to become aware of him. "Is that you, Link?" she asked in a voice that seemed to come from far away.

He nodded earnestly. "Yes, miss, it's me. And you're so cold like. Let me take you inside—"

She shook her head with a violence that made Link consign Lady Vere to the deepest section of hell. This had to be her ladyship's doing and no mistake. But why should Miss Margaret even bother to listen to that old harpy?

"I am going home," Margaret was saying.

Link began to expostulate. It was late. It wasn't safe for a lady to walk in the dark alone. She paid no attention but started down the steps of the house. And that was all wrong, too, for even her walk had lost its usual lissome grace.

On the bottom step she stumbled and would have fallen if Link had not been hovering behind her. He caught her arm and urged, "Let me come with you."

For a moment he thought of what old Reddington would say and then the moon sailed from behind its cloud coverings and shone on the tear that was stealing down Miss Margaret's cheek. Seeing this, Link knew he didn't care a fig for Reddington. Let the old belcher dismiss him without a character and see if he cared.

"Don't you worry about that old bat," he said fiercely. "You're going to be the Countess of Longmarsh, so who cares what *she* says?"

"I'm not going to marry Mr. Trenton."

The air went out of Link. He stared at her in stupefication. Then a thought, hard and ugly, began to form in his mind. Had Mr. Trenton hurt her in some way?

"I was a fool to think that such a marriage would take," Margaret whispered. "I was a dolt. An earl and a paid lady's companion? I was rainbow-chasing."

Trenton *had* played her false. The grand gentleman had been trifling with Miss Margaret, and now he'd spurned her. Link swore an awful oath that he'd make the bugger pay for making the lady cry.

Margaret found her handkerchief and wiped her eyes. Determinedly, she raised her chin and smiled, and the smile broke the young underfootman's heart.

"Oh, miss," he begged, "let me do something. *Please* let me."

For an answer she put her small, cold hand on his. "If you escorted me home, you would be missed. Reddington would ask all sorts of questions and—and I couldn't bear being gossiped about." Her eyes met his. "Nobody must know about—about *anything*, my friend. You understand?"

He understood, all right, Link thought.

She had called him her friend. As he watched her walk away from the house, she looked so lovely and frail and alone. Link swore that he would die rather than betray her trust in him.

He bit his lower lip to stop it from shaking. She had said there was nothing he could do, but there was one thing, and he meant to do it even if it was the last thing he ever did. And he wouldn't regret it—no, not even if he hanged for it.

"Fool. Gudgeon. Dolt."

Margaret called herself even harder names as she stumbled down the dark road homeward. Only it wasn't home any longer, and she had no idea where she and her mother could go.

She knew she had to address that problem, but her mind kept skittering back to what Trent's friends had said and the tone in which they had spoken. And they had been right. In spite of the example of her own mother's life, she had allowed herself to believe that love was enough.

No one had loved each other more than her parents, yet their marriage had produced the bitter fruit of alienation and poverty and sickness. Her mother's family had cut her off for eloping with Captain Hannay, and as a child Margaret had watched her mother's eyes fill with tears at the thought of the sisters and a brother and the parents she would never see again. And when Captain Hannay had died . . .

"I am a fool," Margaret told the listening darkness. "I knew what might happen. I knew why I could not fall in love with Trent."

But she had loved him. She loved him still. And

it was because she loved him that she felt so desperate.

"If I stay here, he won't take no for an answer," Margaret mourned. "He'll tell me it doesn't matter what anyone says. And he'll believe it—or at least he will believe it *now*. But later . . ."

She broke off to wipe away some hen-hearted tears that were rolling down her cheeks. It was incredible to think that she'd been so happy a few hours ago. She was paying for that happiness now.

If she let Trent have his way and marry her, people of consequence would cut him. Only toad-eaters would receive him, and even they would joke about him behind his back. His family would reject him, as would his best friends.

Margaret covered her face with her hands as she thought of Monty's shock and Button's contempt. *Never,* she thought. I'll never let that happen.

But how could she get away safely? Margaret tried to cudgel her brains into action. At the ball there had been so many people. Surely she could find employment with one of them. There was a neighbor, Mrs. Yarrey, Squire Yarrey's wife. She had looked to be a kind, motherly woman, and she had said that she needed a governess for her younger children. For a moment Margaret felt hopeful, but then she realized that the Yarreys would not serve. Their property was too close at hand, and Trent would surely find her there.

She stopped walking and began to murmur names aloud. "Lady Rovermount?" No. Too close. "Mrs. Harrity?" No. "Colonel Bracey?"

"Eh?" a male voice said gruffly.

Margaret nearly jumped out of her skin. She was so nervous and upset that she missed the alarm in the voice as it continued, "Who's there? Who wants me?"

Poised for flight, Margaret's trembling legs failed her. She stood rooted to the spot as Colonel Bracey of the dragoon guards materialized out of the shadows of the topiary garden. His enormous mustache seemed to quiver with agitation and around him clung the undeniable smell of a cigar.

"Ha! Hum!" Colonel Bracey coughed. "Ah, Miss Hanney. I expect that my good lady sent you after me, what?" Margaret shook her head wordlessly. "Didn't?" the colonel demanded. "Oh, er, very good. I thought that she'd . . . I see. Very good."

He seemed to breathe more easily. Clasping his hands behind his back, he surveyed Margaret somewhat sternly.

"What are you doing out here at this time of night, ma'am? Alone, too. By gad, that's not done at all," he lectured her.

Margaret tried to talk and couldn't. The colonel took another look at her face and frowned. "What's the matter?" he asked.

It was the kindness in his gruff voice that proved her undoing. Until then she had had herself reasonably under control. Now the tears welled up in her eyes again. The colonel's gray eyebrows shot up.

"Something's distressing you!" he exclaimed. "Tell me what it is. What? Can't have Percy Hannay's daughter distressed, can I?" He slid a confiding arm through hers. "Let's walk back to the house and you can tell me on the way."

"No," Margaret whispered.

"No? Well, by gad, that's very odd." The colonel twisted one end of his mustache and repeated, "Don't you want to go back to the house?"

"No, sir."

"Have you, ah, reason not to want to return there?"

Resolutely Margaret said, "A very good reason, sir. I've given Lady Vere notice."

The colonel digested this for a moment. "Tell me the whole," he said then. "Wait a bit, there's a seat here. Sit down, Miss Hannay, and tell me what happened."

He conducted her to the seat under the eagle—the seat on which earlier she had sat with Trent as they planned and dreamed and kissed. Margaret forced that thought away and told the colonel what had occurred. He did not interrupt her, but he twisted first one and then the other end of his mustache and made rusty rumbles in his throat.

When she had finished, he regarded her solemnly for some time. "So you've left Lady Vere's employ," he summarized. "What? And you need a new position. Is that it?"

"Yes, sir. If you know of someone who needs a companion or a governess . . ."

"I don't," he replied bluntly.

Margaret's hopes tumbled about her ears. "Oh," she murmured. Rising to her feet, she added, "I'm sorry for detaining you, sir. I'll bid you good night."

"Humgudgeon." The colonel snorted. "You didn't let me finish. Ladies," he added somewhat plaintively, "never do. What? Even my good lady is always butting in when I have just come to the point I want to make. I'm glad that you are leaving Lady Vere."

Margaret stared at him.

"A well-brought-up girl like you—coming from a fine family—Percy Hannay's daughter, don't you know," the colonel went on earnestly, "could have been my own daughter if my good lady and I'd been blessed with children, which, unfortunately, we weren't. What? A girl like you shouldn't have to scrabble about for her bread."

Colonel Bracey broke off and nodded decisively. "My good lady and I spoke of it together tonight. We agreed that you and Mrs. Hannay deserve far better than Lady Vere. Hate to say it of our hostess, but she's common."

"Oh," Margaret murmured rather faintly.

The colonel peered at her shadowed face and said earnestly, "I beg you don't take offense. What? But when we visited Mrs. Hannay today, she and my good lady rubbed along so famously, that my good lady begged your mother to visit us. Begged her with tears in her eyes."

The colonel shot to his feet, gave Margaret an old-fashioned bow, and said somewhat stiffly, "I hope that you and Mrs. Hannay will consider coming to the Welsh border to stay with us."

"To the Welsh border!" exclaimed Margaret.

He misinterpreted her expression. "I realize it is an out-of-the-way place. What? Far from London and all the excitement that young people crave. My lady and I live a quiet life, I fear. A bit of a pond stocked with trout, some horses, and a rose garden. My good lady has been lonely, you know," he confided, "and I thought that dear old Hannay's widow, don't you know . . ." He let his words trail away.

Margaret was hardly conscious of getting to her feet or of clasping her hands together. "Colonel Bracey, *please* take us away," she begged.

Then she burst into tears. The colonel, after staring at her with his mouth half open for several seconds, acted in a manner that did credit to the dragoon guards. He put a fatherly arm about her, patted her several times on the back, and told her firmly that everything would work out for the best.

"Assure you . . . By gad, my good lady will be delighted. We'll leave in the morning."

"Mayn't we leave now?" Margaret begged.

"Now? You mean this minute? Well, mean to say, awkward, what with my lady and your mother. What? Can't expect ladies to put things together in a few hours. Not like the military," he added. "In the old days, my batman could pack up in ten minutes. I was at Corunna, you know."

"So was my father," Margaret said. The events of the evening had taken on a dreamlike quality. Could any of this be happening? she wondered, and hoped that it was.

"Dear old Hannay. Well, well. I know that I'll have many good talks with your mother," said the colonel happily. "We'll leave tomorrow after breakfast, providing it's agreeable with your lady mother."

He advised her to return home and acquaint Mrs. Hannay with what had happened. He would, he added, inform his wife. If he felt that Mrs. Bracey might be surprised at the thought of a sudden departure at the break of dawn, he did not say so. He also cut short Margaret's fervent thanks.

"No thanks necessary. What? The joy this news is going to give my good lady is more than I'd hoped for."

He insisted on walking her home to the cottage, which he surveyed with profound disapproval, saying that he was shocked that Lady Vere was such a squeeze-purse as to lodge Percy Hannay's widow and daughter in such a ramshackle habitation. Then he bowed, begged Margaret to give his compliments to Mrs. Hannay and to make sure it would not inconvenience her to be ready at dawn.

He had begun to march back down the path when he suddenly stopped and turned. "Miss Hanney . . ."

He had changed his mind. Margaret's heart gave a painful thump.

"I'd appreciate it if you didn't tell my good lady about my blowing a cloud," the colonel said. He lowered his voice. "Not supposed to smoke cigars. Confounded medical man says so. He's a duffer, but unfortunately my good lady believes everything the quack says."

Margaret breathed again. "I won't say a word," she promised.

He brightened. "By gad, you sound just like old Hannay. Sensible man! Game as a pebble!" He bowed. "Till tomorrow, ma'am."

Margaret watched him go. The relief that had

buoyed her till now slowly collapsed upon itself like a balloon emptied of air.

She knew that she should be grateful. By great good fortune, she had managed to find a haven for herself and her mother. And by even greater good fortune, that place was far away.

"Trent will never find me there," Margaret murmured. "He doesn't know Colonel Bracey. He won't know where to look for me. And it's for the best. I will make do—I will make do without Trent."

But for once Russkin's old dictum brought her no comfort.

A shadowed figure silhouetted against the greater dark, Link slithered out of the back door of Vere Hall. Ears primed to every night noise, he made his way through the herb garden in back of the hall and approached the storehouse. There he paused and listened before creeping up to the big wooden door.

There was a formidable chain and an enormous padlock on the door, but these did not deter Link from his purpose. As he began to pick the lock, he tried not to think about the penalty for burglary. And anyway, he reassured himself, it wasn't as if he were going to keep anything. He just needed to *borrow* the late master's blunderbuss.

The storehouse padlock clicked open. Gritting his teeth, Link tried to withdraw the chain. It gave a horrible grinding shriek that would have awakened the dead.

Nervously looking around him, Link pulled the chain away and turned the doorknob to the storeroom. The hinges of the door squealed as he pushed it back to disclose a dark, cavernous, musty-smelling storehouse.

"Quickly now," he encouraged himself quietly. "Softly, Peter. That's the ticket."

He was sweating and his hands shook so much that at first he couldn't light the candle he'd brought along. Finally he got it lit, and holding it high, he looked around him at the bundles and boxes that were stored there. "It should be hanging on that wall," Link muttered, "and there it is."

He had just reached up to take the blunderbuss off the wall when Reddington's voice snarled, "Stand where you are!"

Link's jump nearly took him out of his shoes. He turned and saw a truly awesome sight. Reddington was wearing a white-and-red-striped nightcap and was encased in a nightshirt that covered him from neck to midcalf. By the light of the lantern he carried, he looked like an outraged whale.

"I knew you were up to no good," Reddington sneered. "Now, my lad, it's gaol for you and transportation at the very least. Or they may hang you." He added with relish, "You'll be hanged by the neck until you strangle—or until some good friend comes and pulls your legs so that you can die easier."

Link acted from sheer terror. Dropping his candle, he snatched the blunderbuss from the wall and flailed out with it in the general direction of the butler.

Reddington gave a roar of surprise, and in avoiding Link's desperate blow, he dropped his lantern. The next moment, he was sitting with his bare backside on the storehouse floor.

Link darted outside. Reddington attempted to get up but fell backward when he heard the storehouse door slam. There was the rattle of a key being turned in the lock.

"Link!" Reddington bellowed. "You thatchgallows, come back here!"

But the underfootman was hastily putting distance between himself and the butler's muffled cries.

Dawn was already painting the sky. If his luck held, Link thought, the old bubble would stay undiscovered till morning. That would give him enough time to find Mr. Trenton, make him confess his crimes against Miss Margaret, and shoot him dead.

Chapter Eleven

$\mathscr{I}$t was, Trent thought, a magnificent morning.

Last night, after leaving Vere Hall, he hadn't wanted to go to bed. Instead he had ridden through what remained of the night, traversing meadow and brook and hill without the slightest idea as to where he was going.

Margaret was all he could think about. In his imagination he held her again in his arms. In memory he kissed her soft lips. He thought of the look in her eyes and of her smile and of the love words spoken in her sweet voice.

"She loves me," Trent informed a blackbird on a nearby hedge. "She really loves me.'

He felt in his pocket, drew out the rose she had worn in her hair, and raised it to his lips. The flower carried the fragrance of her hair, and when he held it against his cheek, he could feel the velvet of her lips.

My love.

Here he was, talking to birds and kissing flowers. He knew he was acting like a bedlamite, but he didn't care. Nor did his remaining months of servitude weigh heavily on him. Trent even felt grateful toward his great-uncle. If the old duffer had not forced him to come to Longmarsh, he might never have met the one woman in the world who mattered.

"If I'd stayed in London, I'd never have known she existed," Trent mused. "I might have kept on dangling after Lavinia Jerryham. Lord, what a thought that is. Last night, when she was furious with me, she looked just like her mother."

Beau whickered as though in agreement, and Trent scratched his ears. "Tired, old fellow? I should think so, the way we've rambled around. Time to go home to breakfast, eh? A rubdown and a bucket of oats for you, and for me scones, kidneys, and eggs—that will do for a start."

But first, even before breakfasting, he must write a letter to his mother. And later in the day he would call on Mrs. Hannay and ask for permission to pay his addresses to her daughter.

Trent didn't feel a bit tired as he trotted his horse through the copse of trees that bordered Longmarsh. Pausing for a moment, he looked about at the lush green meadows dotted with sheep and at farmland brave with rye and wheat. He regarded the familiar territory fondly, then thought of Margaret again.

She would be the ideal mistress for Longmarsh: fair, loyal, and beloved by all who served her. Last night she had outshone all of Lady Vere's guests with her beauty and her quality, and he'd been hard put not to shout out his news when he'd brought her back to the great hall. When he'd danced with Margaret through the night, he'd seen Montesque and Button staring. They'd understand soon enough, however, and Margaret would take her rightful place in the world as the Countess of Longmarsh.

Trent's thoughts trailed away as he approached his cottage and saw Howard Block's landaulet standing by the gate. A stream of smoke was coming from the cottage chimney, a sure sign that the elderly woman who came to "do" for him each day was at work. Block was probably having it cheerful with eggs and kidneys by now. But what had brought him here at this hour?

Trent wondered about this as he took Beau into the small stable next to the cottage, rubbed him down, and gave him his feed. Then he went inside.

"What's to do, Mr. Block?" he began, then stopped when he saw that the land steward wasn't alone. A spare figure was seated by the grate sipping a glass of sherry.

"Mr. Palchard!" Trent exclaimed.

The solicitor rose and bowed creakily. "I hope I find you well, sir," he said.

"You find me surprised," Trent admitted.

Block cleared his throat. "I beg your pardon for making ourselves comfortable while you were gone, sir, but we had no idea how long you might be, and I took the liberty ..." He bowed and raised the glass of sherry he held. "Mr. Palchard, you see, was in need of a restorative after his journey from London."

"Spirits are known for their curative powers," the lawyer said in his dry way. "I hope you do not mind?"

"Of course not. But why—"

"Surely you are hungry?" Howard Block interrupted. "I will tell Rachel to hurry the breakfast along. Weldon naturally wished to accompany

Mr. Palchard, but he needed time to pack your effects. He will follow shortly to serve you, my lord earl."

"You're going too fast for me." Trent tossed down his riding crop and added, "Begin at the beginning, please, and tell me why Weldon—*What* did you call me?"

Both men spoke in unison. "May I be the first to salute you as the Earl of Longmarsh?" Block intoned, while the little solicitor said simultaneously, "I hope I am the first to felicitate your lordship."

"You mean that I—"

"You have not only succeeded to the title, my lord," Palchard said, "but have also inherited all the monies due you by the terms of the late earl's will."

There seemed to be a ringing in Trent's ears. "But the year isn't up," he protested.

Again Palchard and Block spoke at the same time. "The Time has been waived, my lord—"

Block said. Palchard explained, "By the terms of your great-uncle's will, my lord—"

They both broke off and regarded each other coldly.

"I believe," Palchard snapped, "that it is my place to explain matters to his lordship."

Block looked indignant. "As his lordship's land steward, it is incumbent upon me to do the honors."

"Will you tell me what's going on?" Trent demanded. Both men began to speak at once. "No, don't do that again. Mr. Palchard, please explain."

The lawyer shot a smug look at Block. Smoothing his hands over his coat, he began, "You are naturally aware of the terms of your great-uncle's will. Although the title was due to you by right, the late earl made you his sole heir to his unentailed fortune only on condition that you would come to Longmarsh, begin work as a groom—"

("Come to the point," Block begged under his breath.)

"—and then take on the duties of assistant land steward. These things he did for several reasons. Perhaps you can guess what these reasons were, my lord?"

("Incredible. *Now* he is playing guessing games.")

"I cannot continue if there are ... interruptions!" Palchard complained, and Trent hurriedly interposed.

"I gather you mean that my great-uncle wanted me to learn about the estate before stepping into his boots."

Palchard beamed. "Exactly right, your lordship," he crowed.

"And," Block interjected before Palchard could continue, "he felt that a good master must know his servants."

"His lordship is aware of all that," Palchard said testily.

Ignoring the solicitor, Block bowed deeply to Trent. "Forgive me, my lord, but since your great-uncle was gracious enough to confide his plan to me long before he even wrote his will, I feel that I must speak."

Block touched the tips of his fingers together, rocked back on his heels, and launched into what was obviously a prepared address.

"My lord, I have had the honor of being the land steward to the late Earl of Longmarsh for thirty years. I pray that I will, ah, acquit myself satisfactorily in your service for a long a time. My late master never had grounds to complain of me, and I shall endeavor to make certain that you, too, will not."

("Pish," muttered Palchard. "Is the fellow running for public office?")

"His lordship the late earl," Block continued, "was not a well man during his last months. One evening he called me in. 'Block,' he said, 'I will soon quit this earth. I am grateful that most of my relatives have pre-deceased me since none of them was of any earthly use.' I beg your pardon, my lord," Block broke off to add, "but those were the late earl's sentiments, not mine."

"Go on."

" 'Block,' my late master continued, 'I had one relative who married an opera singer. Another was such a prig that he gave me the megrims. And my only surviving nephew is totty-headed. All he thinks about are horses, his ne'er-do-well friends, and chasing lightskirts.' "

"Is it necessary," Palchard demanded hotly, "to give the late earl's precise words?"

"His late lordship's sentiments were, ah, the cause of the terms of his will. The late earl felt that he could not allow Mr. Trenton to inherit the estate immediately. 'I can't run the risk of having young Trenton turning my estate into a bear garden,' my late master said. 'He's a good enough boy but left to his own devices, he'll let it go to rack and ruin. *He* won't care a hang for it except that it'll give him the blunt for ladybirds and expensive horses and to keep his demmed gambling friends off Queer Street.' Then he added, 'But if he learns to know the land and the people on the land, if he comes to love Longmarsh, *then* he may do very well.' "

Palchard began to expostulate. The land steward continued his speech. Into the ensuing noise Trent roared, "Silence!"

There was instant quiet. "Am I to understand," Trent said slowly, "that I've satisfied my great-uncle's requirements? A yes or no answer," he added sternly as both men began to speak.

"Yes, my lord," Palchard said.

"For various reasons, the time of my, er, apprenticeship has been reduced?"

"Yes, my lord. When Mr. Block wrote to me and informed me of your progress, I hastened to draw up the necessary papers."

Trent drew a deep breath. "Do I understand that I am now the Earl of Longmarsh with all the unentailed money from my late great-uncle's fortune at my command?"

"There are some formalities, but in essence, my lord, you have the right of it."

"Good God!" Trent exclaimed. He sank down in a chair and was silent for several moments. "This changes everything."

"But of course, my lord." Block beamed. "You will no doubt wish to meet your staff and, ah, effect some changes before taking residence at Longmarsh Manor."

"Eh? Oh, yes. I wasn't thinking of that." Trent had begun to smile. What he *was* thinking about was that he needed to pay a visit to the soon-to-be Countess of Longmarsh.

But it was some time before he could carry out this plan. First, both his solicitor and his land steward insisted on conducting an enormous amount of business. Besides the legal documents that required his signature, there were books and ledgers that Block insisted he examine.

"For though you are already quite familiar with your estate, my lord, you do not know all the details," he explained.

The details took all morning, and by afternoon Trent was feeling light-headed. The elderly tyrants permitted him to eat a hearty luncheon but immediately afterward put him to work again. It was not until midafternoon that Block and Palchard finally accompanied Trent to Longmarsh Manor. Here the astonished Gowan was told to convene all of the household and outdoors servants in the great hall.

Trent was aware of the hum of astonishment that grew in volume as he casually walked through the crowded hall. He could hear Jennings asking sullenly, "Wot's 'e think e's up ter?"

Then, as he faced his servants, Trent found that his light-headedness had vanished. In its stead came an odd sense of rightness. He now realized that if he had come straight from London to take over the reins at Longmarsh, he would not have known what to do. He would have felt unsure as he addressed the assembled servants.

He spoke with calm certainty. "I am the Earl of Longmarsh. The late earl was my great-uncle." A gasp punctuated by a yelp from Jennings interrupted him. He paused for a moment before adding, "For many reasons, I came here among you in an unorthodox way."

Trent stopped and looked around the great hall. His eyes met each man's and woman's. The cook blanched and dropped his eyes. Jennings looked ready to have convulsions on the spot. The insolent footman seemed ready to cry. Others, like Ormsby, the housekeeper, and Gowan looked astounded but pleased.

"I have come to know all of you," Trent continued. "I will now decide which of you will remain in my employ." He turned to Jennings, adding, "I begin with you. You have mishandled and mismanaged the late earl's horses and his trust, Jennings. You are dismissed."

Jennings opened his mouth to curse, saw the look on the new earl's face, and turned pale instead. "Yer lordship—" he whined.

Trent interrupted coldly, "Collect your things and take yourself off, or I will personally kick you off my property."

Trent did not watch the former head groom slink away. Instead, he continued to speak to the rest of his staff. Watching, Palchard was well pleased. The old earl had been a downy one and no mistake, he thought. If he contrasted Mr. Trenton's behavior when first told of the will to his attitude now . . .

"He is every inch a lord," Block murmured proudly.

For once in agreement, Palchard nodded. "That he is, sir. Longmarsh will rest comfortably in his hands. Though, of course, it lacks a mistress. His lordship is young, however. No doubt he will not consider it necessary to marry and fill his nursery at so early a date."

Block smiled loftily. "That's all *you* know!"

Some time later, the new Earl of Longmarsh rode toward the tumbledown cottage inhabited by the Hannays. Considering the fact that he had not slept in thirty-six hours, he was in high fettle. He had stopped in a field to pick a bouquet of daisies and dandelions, and now he held this posy in front of him like an offering.

"Madam," Trent began, "I beg that you will allow me to pay my addresses to your daughter. No, that's too stiff by half. Madam, I love your daughter and wish with all my heart to make her my countess. Hell and the devil, that's terrible—makes me sound like a damned actor on the stage." He ruffled his glossy black hair in an agony of indecision. "Plague take it," he complained, "what can I say that doesn't make me sound like a chucklehead?"

He was approaching the tumbledown cottage now, and Trent gave way to daydreams. In a few moments Margaret would open the door and come out to meet him, her hands outstretched and that heartstopping smile on her lips. He would kiss her hand and tell her his news, and then they would go to see her mother together.

"Mrs. Hannay," Trent cried, inspired, "I love your daughter. I've asked her to marry me, and she's made me the happiest man in the world by accepting me. But we need you to come and live with us at Longmarsh."

By now he was at the door of the cottage, but

the door remained shut. Hadn't Margaret heard him yet?

Perplexed, Trent dismounted and knocked on the door. There was no immediate answer, but he thought he heard a step within. "Margaret?" he called.

Still no answer, but now he thought he heard a mumble behind the door. "Mrs. Link?" he queried.

The door cracked open, and a scared voice hissed, "Go away, sir, please!"

Had something happened to Margaret or her mother? Trent gave the door a vigorous push, and it flew open.

"Don't, Peter, oh, don't!" Mrs. Link wailed.

Trent found himself face-to-face with the business end of a blunderbuss. "Now I has you," Link snarled. "You can't escape."

"Why are you pointing that thing at me?" Trent demanded wrathfully.

"Damn you." Link slammed the cottage door shut with one hand while keeping Trent covered with the weapon. "She's gone where you can't hurt her no more."

"Do you mean to tell me Miss Hannay's gone?" Mrs. Link threw her apron over her head and began to wail and moan. "Where's she gone to, Mrs. Link?"

"Move a muscle and you're a dead man," Link hissed.

Trent ignored him. "Where, Mrs. Link?"

"She's gone, the pretty lady," Mrs. Link wept.

Trent turned to Link. "Will you put that damned thing down?"

"I won't. You hurt Miss Margaret and made her cry," Link cried.

"Margaret *crying*? Why was she crying?"

There was so much wrath, astonishment, and dismay in Trent's voice that Link's purpose wavered. But it weakened only for a moment. When he thought of the poor lady's tears last night, he could have pulled the trigger right then and there. He would, too, an' all. But first, this wicked gentleman had to know why he was being executed.

"She were crying acourse o' you, that's why!" Link shouted. "She told me, she did, that a match between the likes o' you couldn't be. You lied to her and—"

Link yelped as, moving with a blur of speed, Trent struck the weapon aside. The blunderbuss discharged, sending shot spraying through roof and window. Mrs. Link screamed as Trent leaped on Link, knocked him down, and seized the blunderbuss.

"Sir, oh, sir, don't kill my boy," Mrs. Link wailed.

Trent flung the blunderbuss into a corner of the room. "I'm going to tear him apart if he doesn't tell me what's going on." He bent down, hauled up the underfootman by the collar, and shook him till his teeth rattled. Squawking dismay, Mrs. Link clutched Trent's arm.

"I'll tell, sir, I'll tell. Miss Margaret and Mrs. Hannay went away this morning, sir, with Colonel Bracey and his lady. They was heading toward the Welsh border."

"The Welsh— But, my God, *why*?"

Link choked, "Acourse she loves you, you

bugger. You broke her heart. Making her love you and then showing as you was going ter be an earl and too good for the likes of her. She heard yer Lunnon friends talking, she did, and she knew you was trifling with her—"

Trent set Link back on his feet. His green eyes burned. "Tell me everything," he said in a deadly voice. It was a voice to inspire fear in a much braver heart than Peter Link's. But even though his teeth chattered with terror, Link shook his head.

"Man, I *love* her," Trent roared.

Link wavered. "But she said—"

The door crashed open. Trent, his hands still locked about Link's throat, whirled to face the fierce, quivering, beet-red countenance of Reddington.

"Miscreant!" Reddington howled.

Lady Vere's butler carried a walking stick in his shaking hand. He pointed it at Link. Behind him crowded Nancy, Mrs. Pollyshot, Elsie, and Noah.

"Wretch! Knave! Thief!" With every new epithet, Reddington's wattles turned a darker red. "Mr. Trenton, I see you have apprehended the criminal. I beg you will hand him over to me. Cook has gone for the officers of the law."

Mrs. Link gave a loud squawk and fell backward in a faint. "Mam!" Link shouted, but Trent would not let him go.

"Explain," he snapped at Reddington.

The butler was only too glad to do so. His dignity had never been so abused. He still writhed when he thought of how he had been found by

Nancy this morning, huddled in his nightshirt, hoarse with shouting.

"Not only did he steal that blunderbuss, sir, but he came here to murder you. He must be put in irons immediately." Reddington added with relish, "I do not doubt that he will be hanged."

Mrs. Link, who had been coming to, fell back in a second faint. Nancy slipped past the butler and knelt beside the prostrate woman. Elsie and Mrs. Pollyshot followed suit.

"Mr. Reddington, there's no need fer such talk," the housekeeper reproved. "You've frightened this poor soul into a fit."

"And there's no need for the law," Trent added. His brain, deprived of sleep and subjected to a succession of shocks, had finally been jogged into working order. "No need at all. You see, Link came to assist me."

"To assist *you*?" Reddington goggled. So did Link.

"He'd heard that I was about to set out after Miss Hannay and her mother, and he borrowed the blunderbuss to protect us. You know what the roads to the Welsh border are like."

"Dangerous they are," Nancy cut in. "Decent souls shouldn't be riding along on them unarmed."

Reddington seemed to be on the point of having a seizure. "Do you mean to tell me that Link came to assist you to recover Miss Hannay? But—but there was the sound of a shot."

"The thing went off accidentally. It's in a bad condition," Trent went on sternly. "You should be more careful with these antique weapons, Reddington. Your carelessness could have caused a fatal accident." He picked up the blunderbuss and shoved it at Lady Vere's staring butler. "Take the damned thing home and make sure it's stored someplace safe this time."

"But," Reddington persisted triumphantly, "Link is not your servant, sir. He is in Lady Vere's service and under my orders—"

"Not anymore," Trent said promptly. "He's employed at Longmarsh Manor as a footman. I've sacked the current one. He was impudent, and I'll stand for no impudence on *my* staff, Reddington."

The words, spoken with awful severity, left no room for doubt. "Lawks," Elsie gasped. "Do that mean—"

" 'E's an h'earl h'already," Mrs. Pollyshot squealed. "Oh, dearie, dearie me!"

Link fell at Trent's feet, blabbering, "Forgive me, yer worship. I didn't realize what were going on. I thought—"

He was interrupted by Trent, who begged him to stubble it. "You were ready to do anything to help Miss Hannay. I'd forgive the devil himself for that." He looked about him at the assembled servants, adding, "As a matter of fact, I don't doubt that the future countess will want all those loyal to her to follow her to Longmarsh. With better wages, of course."

Ignoring Reddington's strangled gasp, Trent turned back to Link. "You know the route Colonel Bracey took? Excellent. Get a horse from my stables. We leave immediately."

Link sped to the door but was halted by Reddington. "Sir—I mean, my lord—I must protest," he began.

"Well, don't."

"This man offered me violence."

"What he means," Nancy said impudently, "is that he were locked up in the storehouse in his nightshirt. With his bare bum showing."

Everyone, even Mrs. Link, burst out laughing, and Reddington collapsed like a perforated bladder.

Trent pushed past the speechless Reddington and strode outside. A quick glance at the sun showed that it would set in a few hours. "They'll lay over at an inn along the way," he muttered. "I can catch up to them if I ride all night." Hoofbeats behind him made him add, "By God, Link, you're very quick."

"What the deuce are you talking about, dear old boy?"

Trent swiveled. "You!" he exclaimed in accents of loathing.

" 'Pon my word," Montesque protested. "What in blazes is wrong with you? Help! He's gone mad!"

"Get down, you bloated toad." Trent seized Montesque's boot and attempted to drag him from the saddle. Montesque just as grimly clung to it. "Get down and face me like a man. I'm calling you out!"

"Calling Monty out?" Button had just ridden up in a curricle and was staring in pop-eyed astonishment. "What has come over you, old fellow?"

"I'm calling you out, too. You dared to speak to Miss Hannay, didn't you? You convinced her that a match between us wouldn't fadge."

"Speak to Miss Hannay?" burbled Montesque.

"Been in the sun too long, Trent? Takes a fellow strangely, does the sun. Of course we didn't talk to Miss Hannay about such a thing. Definitely not ton."

"Do you think we would be such cads?" Button demanded. "Cool down, there's a good fellow."

Montesque made soothing noises. In a cold, deadly voice, Trent asked, "You didn't talk to Miss Hannay?"

"Give you my word," Montesque said. "Just left Korrowin's. Miss Lakehart tried to kiss Button."

Button's long frame shivered in every joint. "It was a horrible experience, my dear fellow. I pray you will not mention it to a soul. But as you can see, it would be impossible to remain at Norsby under the circumstances. Monty and I were riding for London forthwith and wished to say goodbye. Now we see you in distress. What is the matter?"

In a few, terse words, Trent explained the situation. His friends looked at each other in dismay.

"Must have overheard us last night," Montesque said gloomily. "Now don't fly up in the boughs, Trent, we didn't mean for her to overhear. We were just saying that it would be a mismatch, you being an earl and she a lady's companion. But then we changed our minds."

"On the road back to Norsby, don't you know," Button added. "What Monty means is that we thought it through and decided that a fine woman like Miss Hannay—not her fault, is it, that her father went and got himself killed? Lots of fine ladies are forced to earn their blunt. It's to her credit."

"We think that you shouldn't trifle with her, Trent," Montesque lectured. "Should offer for her, in fact, if she'll have you. Girls like that don't come along but once in a lifetime. Puts Miss Jerryham fair in the shade, give you my word."

Trent was saved from answering by a clatter of hoofbeats and the arrival of Link. He was mounted on Jennings's horse.

"I had ter knock someone out o' the saddle to get this fellow," Link reported. "Big, ugly brute he were and cussed me something orful. I hope I done right, my lord?"

Trent grinned as he mounted Beau. "You'll rise quickly in my service, Link."

"My lord?" Montesque goggled.

"Your service?" Button looked just as pop-eyed. "I say, old fellow, does this mean you've actually succeeded to the title and the—the, er, *money*?"

Just then Mrs. Pollyshot, Mrs. Link, Nancy, Elsie, and Noah, followed by a deflated Reddington, came crowding out of the hut.

Trent spurred Beau onward. "I'll explain later," he shouted over his shoulder.

Montesque stared after the two riders. "Now, if that don't beat all. Never saw such a fellow. Rides off and leaves us hanging. After all we've done for him. Can you make out what happened, dear boy?"

Button sighed. "It seems as if he's made a mull of it and Miss Hannay's gone away. He'll make another mull of it if he's left on his own." Montesque began to shake his head mutinously. "We're his *friends*, Monty. We can't let him ruin his one chance for happiness. Besides, Miss Hannay *did* overhear us speaking and got the wrong idea in her brain-box." Button drew himself up. "We have a responsibility," he announced, "to unite those two."

"Huzzah!" shouted Nancy, Elsie, Mrs. Pollyshot, Noah, and Mrs. Link.

Reddington alone remained silent.

"What if Miss Hannay don't want to be united?" Montesque objected. "Maybe she don't love him, Button. Think of that."

"Monty, you are the most cabbage-brained . . . Don't you know anything? No female goes off and leaves a man because she hates him. It's not done. She has to love him to give him up, don't you see?" Button cracked his whip and added, "Onward!"

"No, I don't see," said Montesque, sighing, but he followed. Glumly.

Chapter Twelve

Mrs. Hannay paused in the midst of a fascinating discussion of country gardens and reached for her daughter's hand. It felt like ice.

"Are you comfortable, dearest?" she asked anxiously.

"Yes, indeed. And you, Mama?"

Margaret's voice sounded normal. Everything about her was controlled. Too controlled, Mrs. Hannay thought.

Mrs. Hannay frowned and wished that her eyes were better so that she could see her daughter's face more clearly. Margaret had been quite calm when she had awakened her in the small hours and described a part of her scene with Lady Vere. Then she had explained Colonel Bracey's offer.

"Lady Vere is malicious enough to evict us immediately, Mama," she had said. "It's best we accept the Braceys' kind offer and go at once."

Mrs. Hannay had not protested. She had been a soldier's wife and was used to sudden moves. Besides, for months she had prayed that it would be possible for her daughter to leave Lady Vere's service.

Now, however, she was worried because something had gone wrong. It had nothing to do with that odious woman, either. Unless she missed her guess, Mrs. Hannay thought shrewdly, it had everything to do with Kenneth Trent—or Trenton, as he called himself these days.

Mrs. Hannay squeezed her daughter's cold hand again, but this time Margaret did not respond.

Margaret was numb. She had felt nothing but a dull ache since their departure several hours ago. Up till the moment of leaving this morning, she had been driven by the fear that Trent would come to the cottage and stop them from leaving. She knew that if she saw him, she might not be strong enough to leave.

But Trent had not come, and the Braceys' chaise had arrived. Margaret had agonized as Mrs. Bracey and her mother greeted each other with exclamations of mutual joy. She had nearly screamed at the slowness with which the Braceys' ancient coachman bestowed the luggage and at the age it took for Mrs. Bracey's abigail to reposition herself. Then, a few miles down the road, one of the chaise's wheels had become stuck in a rut. Two hours later they were properly on their way, and since then Margaret had felt nothing.

She watched the light rain scud like tears across the chaise window and paid scant attention to the elderly ladies, who gossiped happily about mutual friends and memories of military balls. She did not even hear Colonel Bracey's snores.

Instead, she tried to think of a course of action. They couldn't become dependent on their new friends' generosity. That was the way to lose friends. It was a blessing that the ladies dealt so famously with each other, however, for she could leave her mother in good hands while she looked for a position.

With the kindly Braceys as sponsors, Margaret thought, she could also be more selective. Perhaps she could find a family with sweet little children. Life in such a household would be quite pleasant.

The chaise rattled over some stones in the road and the colonel awoke with a start. "Hum," he exclaimed, "ha! Getting dark, I see. You ladies must be fatigued. What? We should put up for the night."

"You remember, my dear," Mrs. Bracey said calmly, "that we decided to spend the night at Burston. We have been much delayed by that unfortunate incident with the wheel, but Burston is not far now."

The colonel, engaged in tweaking his mustache into life, glanced at Margaret's pale face. "You look peaked, Miss Hannay," he said in a rallying tone. "A good dinner, a good fire ... What? And a long rest. By gad, this chaise rattles every bone in one's body."

At this moment there was a hullabaloo outside. Glancing out of the window again, Margaret saw that they had just passed the London coach.

Mrs. Bracey was immediately concerned. "The driver of that coach seems to be making for Burston, too. That means the inn will be overcrowded. If we cannot bespeak a private parlor and bedrooms, we may need to push on to Manfred-on-Heath."

An animated discussion followed. Mrs. Hannay, who was actually exhausted, professed herself to be not at all tired and eager to push on if this was what the Braceys wished. Mrs. Bracey owned herself ready to travel a few more miles than be cramped in an odious fashion. Colonel Bracey, pulling out a pocket watch, confessed that he was as hungry as a bear and unable to wait much longer for his dinner.

"Leave it to me, my love," he told his wife, "and I will manage matters. John will get us to the inn long before the coach, and the landlord'll have us all situated in a few minutes. *I* know how to bivouac in inhospitable terrain, and— By gad, what's to do? I thought we left the stage far behind."

Hoofbeats were approaching rapidly. Margaret, peering out the rain-beaded window, saw that two horsemen were urging their mounts forward. As she watched, one of them gave a shout and pointed at the Braceys' chaise.

"Upon my soul," the colonel exclaimed, "those fellows seem to be pursuing us."

"But why, Horatio?" Mrs. Bracey suddenly looked stricken. "Can they be highwaymen?"

Mrs. Hannay gasped and drew closer to her daughter. The colonel scowled and, rapping sharply on the chaise roof, commanded his coachman not to spare the whip. The chaise surged forward, bouncing its occupants about like chestnuts in a hot pan.

"Don't fear, ladies," the colonel exclaimed. "We'll outrun the miscreants!"

But the two horsemen had also increased their speed and were thundering after the Braceys' chaise. Margaret, clutching her mother's hand, thought rapidly. They had nothing of value with them, no money to speak of, and the Braceys were traveling light. If these two riders were highwaymen, would they be satisfied with a meager take? She had heard of robbers turning ugly when their prey had insufficient goods.

The same thought must have occurred to the colonel, for he popped his head out of the window and shouted, "Go faster, John! Make the horses fly."

"They're gaining," Mrs. Bracey moaned.

Colonel Bracey began to puff and blow like an old warhorse.

"No help for it. Make a stand, what?" He thumped his stick on the floor. "I'll make mincemeat of those dastards with my sword-stick."

Mrs. Bracey let out a faint shriek. "You'll do no such thing. Horatio, those are dangerous men."

As she spoke, one of the riders overtook them. He swung around and caught the horses' reins. "Stop the chaise!" he ordered.

The old coachman attempted to beat the invader off, and Mrs. Bracey's abigail struck at him with her umbrella. All this was to no avail. Now the second rider rode alongside, and Margaret's heart catapulted into her throat as she recognized Trent.

Before she could react, the chaise jolted to a bone-crunching stop. Mrs. Hannay was flung on top of Margaret, and Mrs. Bracey hurtled on top of them both. Amidst this confusion, the colonel pushed open the door and hopped outside.

"Wait," Margaret cried, trying to extricate herself, "oh, please, stop. It's Trent!"

The colonel did not hear her. He extended his sword-stick and struck a dueling pose. "You touch these ladies over my dead body, sir," he declaimed.

"Trent?" Mrs. Hannay's voice had suddenly turned hopeful. "What is he doing here, Margaret?"

"He's come after me. Oh, how could he have known how to find me? Unless Mrs. Link—" Margaret broke off as she caught a good look at the man holding the horses. It was Peter Link.

"Come down off your horse and fight, dastard!" Colonel Bracey was roaring.

Trent wheeled Beau around. "Colonel Bracey," he soothed, "there's no cause for alarm."

"Ha, villain! What? How come you to know my name?"

"My name is Kenneth Trenton, sir," Trent said. "I met you yesterday at Lady Vere's ball."

The colonel blinked. The young fellow's face was in darkness, but his voice was familiar. "Are you the one who danced the waltz with Miss Hannay?" he demanded suspiciously.

"Sir, I am." Trent watched the colonel lower the point of his sword-stick. "I've followed you because I must speak to Miss Hannay. Is she in the chaise?"

"Yes, she is," the colonel said just as Margaret exclaimed, "No, I'm not."

Trent slid off his horse and peered through the chaise window. "Miss Hannay," he said formally, "I beg you'll step out of the chaise and allow me a private word."

"No!"

Panic filled Margaret. If she were left alone with Trent, if once she looked into his eyes, she knew her noble resolve would waver.

"Only a word," Trent pleaded. Margaret shook her head violently. "Dash it, you went off without a word to me, and I've driven half the day to catch up to you. Please be reasonable."

Colonel Bracey had commenced to tug at his mustache. "Once ladies have their minds made up, the game is over," he philosophized. "No use appealing to reason, my boy. You are up the River Tick."

Trent gazed fixedly at Margaret's white face. "Very well," he said calmly.

He was giving up. He was going away. Margaret knew she should feel floods of relief but instead felt much more miserable than before.

"Remember that you've forced me to do this." Trent raised his voice and declaimed, "Miss Hannay, will you do me the honor of marrying me?"

Margaret's eyes widened. Her heart had begun to thump and skitter like a mad drum.

"I love you," Trent said in that same carrying voice. "I will devote my life to making you happy."

Mrs. Hannay gave her daughter a poke in the ribs. "Margaret, do you not love him?"

"That's not the point!"

"Quite right," said Mrs. Bracey, coming unexpectedly to Margaret's aid. "The question is, Does the man have prospects? I collect, my dear, that I saw you waltz out of doors with him last night. Highly improper, and unwise as well. You know how tongues wag! If your mama had been there, she would have put a stop to it." The colonel's lady paused, regarded Trent, and added significantly, "You must not throw yourself away on a charming nobody."

As his lordship's new footman, Link hoped he knew his place. He realized that he must keep silent, but his anxiety over Miss Margaret's fate forced him to speak. Clearing his throat, he addressed the night air directly in front of him.

"He ain't no nobody. Mr. Trenton is the new Earl of Longmarsh."

Colonel Bracey's eyes widened, and he whistled. "You don't say. Well, my dear young lady, in that case, what could be better? Certainly you should accept his proposal of marriage."

"No," Margaret said desperately, "I can't marry him. *Because* he's the earl—"

Trent seized the door of the chaise and pulled it open. He stuck his head inside and surveyed Margaret with burning green eyes. "I'll renounce my title."

"Good heavens!" Mrs. Hannay exclaimed, and Colonel Bracey seized Trent's arm.

"Consider, my boy. Take a deep breath and think what you are about. What? No joke, renouncing titles."

Trent did not take his eyes off Margaret. "For your sake, I would do anything. Be anyone. I would even," he added, "be a groom for the rest of my life."

It was too much for Margaret. "Can't you see how impossible you are making it for me?" she wailed. "Trent, it would not *do*."

As she spoke, more hoofbeats sounded, and two new personages arrived on the scene. A rotund rider, spurring ahead of a curricle, drew rein beside the Braceys' chaise.

"Oh, ah, Trent," Montesque puffed, "are we in time?"

Trent stared at his friend in astonishment, but Margaret forestalled speech. In her eagerness to make her point, she tumbled out of the chaise and faced Montesque. "Please tell him that a marriage between us would be unequal," she cried.

Montesque nodded firmly. "It would certainly be that."

"You see!"

"You're much too good for him, Miss Hannay," Montesque continued. "But I beg you to accept him, anyway. The dear old boy would be lost without you, give you my word."

"Indeed, Miss Hannay, I add my pleas to Mr. Montesque's," Button added. His normally languid tones were earnest as he added, "There is no lady in the world that our friend loves as much as he loves you. If you do not accept him, he will make himself so miserable that we would suffer abominably. To spare all of us pain, I beg you to listen to his suit."

Speechless, Margaret stared at Montesque and Button. Trent took off his coat and wrapped it around her shoulders. "I love you," he reminded her tenderly.

"But—"

"Oh, go on, lass, take 'im!"

The booming voice came from the driver of the London coach, which had overtaken the chaise. The coachman drew rein and added in the same stentorian tones, "Good men is 'ard to come by."

213

"And the bleeter's mad in love wi' yer," added a passenger who sat beside the driver. He had drunk too much brandy against the cold and hiccupped loudly as he advised, "Don't look like such a bad cove to me. Best take 'un afore 'e changes 'is mind."

Trent smiled down at Margaret. She looked into his eyes and forgot everything else. The warmth, the tenderness, the laughter reflected in his face filled her heart with joy.

"Well, dear one?" Trent asked gently.

For answer, she held out her cold hands. He took them into his large, strong, warm ones. "I love you so much," she admitted in a low voice.

"And you'll marry me?" Margaret nodded. "Say it. Say 'Yes, I'll marry you, Trent.' "

"Yes, I'll marry you, Trent," Margaret repeated dutifully.

Montesque and Button sighed with relief. Link grinned all over his face. The driver of the London coach, along with his passengers, who had stuck their heads out the coach window, cheered loudly. The inebriated passenger threw his hat into the air and promptly lost it.

"Well, well, well," said the colonel, beaming. He assisted Mrs. Hannay from the chaise and watched benevolently as that lady embraced first her daughter and then Trent. "Bless my soul," he went on. "A bit unorthodox, what? But love will have its day. Reminds me of the time when I myself proposed to you, my dear. It wasn't on the high road, but—"

"I should say not. Horatio, that young man is *kissing* the girl. In front of everyone, too."

Mrs. Bracey's shocked words awoke Margaret

from her trance. She drew away from Trent and looked up at him with laughter trembling in her eyes. "This will not do," she murmured. "You must consider how you are compromising me in public."

"How about in private? And don't tell me you take it back about marrying me. You can't. Too many witnesses will swear that they heard you accept me, and I'll sue you for breach of promise." Then, realizing how many interested eyes were fastened on them, Trent added hastily, "The thing to do is to get to someplace warm and dry where we can drink the health of the future Countess of Longmarsh."

"There's a good inn at Burston," Montesque offered hopefully. "Ripping little place. Good fires, good food. Landlord makes a splendid rum-fustian. He takes twelve eggs, see, and adds beer, puts in a bottle of sherry, and—"

The London coachman stirred to life and smacked his lips. He cracked his whip. "Yah!" he yelled, and his horses plunged forward.

Colonel Bracey started. "By gad," he spluttered indignantly, "that lot will take over the entire inn. John, after them, and do not spare the whip!" He helped Mrs. Hannay back into the carriage, then scrambled himself. "Miss Hannay, I beg you to bestir yourself."

"My fiancée will ride with me, sir," Trent said. He spoke with the dignity and authority befitting an earl, and no one, certainly not the beaming Mrs. Hannay, questioned him about propriety. "Mr. Butterworth is going to lend us his curricle."

"Eh? So I am." Button unfolded himself from

the driver's seat and handed the reins of his grays to his friend. "I'll ride your horse up to the inn, Trent, and order us some dinner. Coming, Monty?"

But Montesque hung back to say shyly, "I wish you most happy, Miss Hannay. And you, dear old boy. Getting more than you deserve, give you my word. But then, the wheel has turned again. Round and round it goes. Mark my words, you're on the upswing."

"What did he mean?" Margaret wondered as Montesque trotted his horse into the mist. "I don't understand."

Trent shook his head. "Monty never makes any sense. Forget him and come here."

Margaret found herself enveloped in strong arms and kissed with singleminded passion. Blissfully, she returned those kisses.

Moments passed during which the moon emerged from tattered clouds and beamed down on the lovers. Finally Trent stirred.

"I suppose we'd best be on our way to that inn, too. You must be cold and tired, my love." Margaret shook her head. "No? Then perhaps, as it's stopped raining, we won't need to go immediately."

Her smile was dazzling, enchanting, and more than a trifle roguish. "No," she agreed. "*Certainly* not immediately."